kevin's

CHRONICLES

PART II

The Aftermath

Ron Leath

ISBN 13: 978-1-7330629-1-6

ISBN-10: 1-7330629-1-2

www.ronleath.com

This is a work of fiction. Names, characters, businesses, places, events, locales, and incidents are either the products of the author's imagination or used in a fictitious manner. Any resemblance to actual persons, living or dead, or actual events is purely coincidental.

WARNING: This writing contains some explicit language and small scenes of violence.

DEDICATION

This book is dedicated to all those who believed in me. A special thanks goes to all of you who read my first two books, Kevin's Chronicles I and Common Kings. Trust me, if it wasn't for you guys, I wouldn't have had the motivation to continue.

Visit www.ronleath.com for

updates and new releases!

Table of Contents

ACKNOWLEDGMENTS

As always, praises and thanks go to God. Secondly, I would like to thank my wife, Ebone for believing in me and giving me great advice. I would also like to thank my kids for rooting me. Although they are too young to read these types of books, they are my number one fans. Thanks to my sister, Keke and my brother Jerry. I love you! I have some close friends who read my first book and encouraged me to continue going. Mariel and Twaskie, special thanks goes to you two! Also, a shout out to my editor, Shatika Turner. Thanks for your hard work.

CHAPTER ONE

Nia

The morning after the shootings…

Nia trembled the entire flight. Her heart was racing, her body was numb and her eyes felt like they weighed a thousand pounds. She manage to dose off once or twice, but the compact, low-cost airliner seats and the rumbling turbulence, made it a fight that she couldn't win. She eventually gave in, open her eyes and focused on the dark skies that rested just outside the tiny window.

Her legs were cramped and 35,000 feet in the sky felt more like a ride at a theme park, yet it still wasn't enough to take her mind off Kevin. When Jessica called her hours earlier to tell her that Kevin had been shot, she immediately went into an anxious panic. She dropped everything to catch an overnight flight from Atlanta to Los Angeles.

She arrived at LAX around seven in the morning, quickly grabbed her bags and gave Jessica a call. "Hey, I'm here," she said to her. "Any word on his condition?"

"Girl, I've been at the hospital for over eight hours," Jessica pouted. "They keep saying they can't let me know anything just yet. All they told me was that he is still alive."

Nia let out an exhale of relief. "Well, that's good."

She turned her head towards the buses for the rental car area. The line was stretched from the buses to nearly the door she was standing near. "Girl, I don't know what time I'm going to get to y'all. It's probably gonna take three hours to get to the damn rental counter."

Nia's frustration was starting to show. She hadn't eaten, used the restroom or done anything since she left Atlanta.

"I got you girl," Jessica said to her. "They not gonna tell me anything soon, so I will come pick you up. It may take me a minute, but I'll be there as fast as I can."

"Ok, cool," she said, heading back into the building. She went to the restroom then came back outside and waited on her.

It was the beginning of the winter, but that L.A. breeze felt so good. It was the only thing that relaxed her.

Her phone rang and it was her fiancé, Greg. However, he was the last person on her mind. She smacked her teeth just before she answered.

"Hello?"

"Nia, where the fuck are you?"

"Please don't start with me, Greg. Didn't I tell you I had to catch a flight to L.A. to see about my friend's brother who was shot? And why you always gotta curse at me?"

She was almost to the point that she hated him. His voice was deep and annoying, and he always had to give a lecture when he spoke. It matched his six foot-five frame.

"Girl, what friend? You told me you don't even talk to no one else out there. And I'm cursing because I think you're lying."

She pulled the phone away from her ear and let him argue with himself. Kevin never treated her that way, and over the last few months, she began to realize she made a mistake by getting this deep into a relationship with Greg. He was sweet when they first met, but after the proposal and moving in together, he became verbally and physically abusive. It had been times where she wanted to seek help, but she feared retaliation since he was a police officer.

They met the very next day after she left Kevin. She was on a plane heading back to Dallas and they sat next to each other. He was on a connecting flight to Atlanta, and they ended up exchanging numbers. Greg was in the process of moving from Los Angeles to Atlanta to work as a police officer in a nearby suburb. Once he settled in, he stayed in contact with Nia and eventually talked her into moving with him. One of the main reasons she agreed to do it was the fact that she was still in love with Kevin and needed somebody in her life to help her get over him. Greg was that person at first. He treated her better than she had ever been treated by a man before. He encouraged her to finish school and she eventually found a job in the medical field.

"What's the dude's name who got shot?" Greg asked because he had already called his cop friends in L.A. and got a rundown on the shootings from the night before.

"Greg, just stop. Please. You don't control me."

"I didn't say I did. Just know I looked into the homicides in L.A. from last night. My partner out there told me that the only murders in the Los Angeles metro area happened in Long Beach County. Somebody named Katrina Jones, Nate Jones, and—"

"I didn't say anything about a homicide, Greg! I said he was shot."

"What's his name, then? I know your ass is lying, Nia. You need to come the fuck home before you piss me off."

Nia hung up on him. She had to keep her phone on just in case Jessica called, otherwise she would've cut it off like she always does.

Jessica pulled up minutes later. She helped Nia put her bags in the trunk and they gave each other a long, emotional hug.

"Girl, I missed you so much," Jessica cried.

Nia nodded. "I missed you too, sis. I can't believe that this happened, and I hate that it took all of this for us to see each other again."

Jessica shrugged her shoulders. "Well, you know, life happens."

Jessica still didn't have an update on Kevin's condition and had her doubts that Kevin would live through it. He looked so lifeless when she saw him on the ground the night before. She didn't want to fill Nia's head with her doubts, though. It was best to wait until they heard from the doctors.

Jessica drove to a breakfast spot off Century. She wasn't in the mood for food but knew they both needed to eat something. Plus, it would be the perfect time to catch up. While sitting at the table, Jessica noticed Nia's restless demeanor. She would look down at her phone and blew out her cheeks each time.

"You ok, Nia?" she asked.

Nia shook her head. "I'm fine, girl. It's just that damn Greg has gotten on my last nerve. I don't love him anymore. He's too controlling and he doesn't even respect me. I coulda stayed with Kevin and deal with his drug life had I known all of this would happen."

Jessica didn't know too much about Greg. Last she remembered, they were doing fine. All she could do now was try to be positive. "Well, Nia, if it's that bad then leave him. And don't blame yourself for leaving Kevin. He was making a lot of bad choices before and after you left him."

"Yeah, but Kevin loved me and I shoulda put my foot down and demanded more from him. I guess I was just emotional because my aunt had just died. That's why I left so fast."

Jessica sighed. "Nia, Kevin had a lot going on involving money. After you left him, we lost contact for a while and then he came around my house outta the blue with a nice, shiny car and a new look. He said that he had gone legit and was living in Long Beach. Things were good but then he threw a party for me and I invited Frank and Mike not knowing the history between them. After that, things went downhill and now we're here. Yesterday, he dodged death a couple of times. He got kidnapped, too."

Nia frowned. "Who kidnapped him?" The story was getting crazier by the second.

Jessica let out a smirk. "It may sound crazy but it was his girlfriend's brother."

Nia looked just as confused as the Nick Young meme. "Girl, what? Did she set him up or something? Is this the same girl that you told me he proposed to?"

"Yep, it's her. Her name is Katrina. See, her brother, Nate, used to be cool with Kevin but then he robbed Kevin and Chris one night. Kevin didn't know how dangerous Nate was. On the night of the robbery, Nate didn't get all the money and Kevin took a couple hundred grand of it. Nate felt like the money was his, so he went through several people to get to Kevin—including his own sister, Katrina."

"So, where the fuck Katrina at now? I guarantee she knows something. I will find her and beat her ass myself."

Jessica inhaled and paused before she spoke. "Nia, it sounds crazy, but Kevin believed with all his heart that Katrina was innocent. I believed her too. I talked to her on the phone minutes before she was shot."

"Huh?" Nia interrupted. "She got shot, too?"

"Yes, the detective called me since I was the last person to talk to her over the phone. They found her shot to death in her condo in Long Beach."

"Wait a minute," Nia said as she raised her eyebrow. "So, her, her brother Nate, and Kevin were all shot last night? This all gotta be connected in some kind of way."

Jessica shook her head. "No, Nate is still alive as far as I know. Kevin and Katrina were the only two shot."

"No, I think he's dead, Jess. Greg said that Katrina Jones and Nate Jones were both killed last night."

"How does he know all this?"

Nia leaned back and wiped her face. "Girl, Greg is a damn stalker. He called his cop friends here in L.A. to try to see who my *friend* was that got shot. That's when he told me."

"This is crazy," Jess said as she exhaled. "I was thinking that Nate was the one who shot Kevin, but if he died last night too, then I don't know what to think. Kevin may have had a lot of enemies."

Nia nodded. "Well, we need answers."

CHAPTER TWO

We were Homeboys

Mike got out of bed around noon the next day. He still didn't know what happened to Kevin nor what Frank's beef with Katrina was. After taking a leak, he walked into the living room and saw Frank lying on the couch.

Frank sat up once he heard Mike's heavy footsteps. "Sup Mike? You good?"

Mike nodded. "Yeah, I'm good. Did you hear from Kevin?"

Frank shook his head then reached over and grabbed a cigarette from the coffee table. "Damn, nigga, didn't I tell you they killed Kevin last night? Katrina's shady ass was setting him up all along, just like we thought."

Mike didn't believe him. He kept an eye on Frank's gun that was on the coffee table. "Well, you still ain't tell me what happened to your hand, bruh."

Frank moved his hand back. "Nigga, you a detective or something? Fuck you asking me all these questions for?"

"My bad," Mike said, tapping his chest as he took a couple of steps back. "I just want to know what really went down."

Frank sat all the way up. He cut the TV on and turned to sports highlights before finally looking over at Mike again. "Look man, when I got to his studio, I found him shot over there by a phone booth. Slim was down the street and I confronted him. He cut me on my damn hand but I was able to pull out my pistol and put a hole in his ass."

Mike's eyes widened. "Bruh, Slim dead?"

"Dead as a muthafuckin' doorknob. You know how I get down, nigga."

Mike nervously looked out the window. "Shit, we gotta be on the move then. If the cops don't come for us, Kareem damn sure will."

"Fuck Kareem and the cops. Ain't nobody gonna know shit. I made my moves quietly."

Frank grabbed his gun and went into his room. He closed the door behind him.

Mike went into the kitchen and fixed a bowl of cereal. While sitting at the dining table, Frank's loud voice carried over and he could hear bits and pieces of his conversation. When he heard Kareem's name, he got up and put his ear to the door.

Kareem was a well-known dope boy from Compton whom they met through Slim years ago. They used to be cool until one of Kareem's homeboys robbed and killed one of their homeboys named Jamarcus. The beef was never settled. Mike was surprised that Frank was on the phone with him.

Mike heard Frank telling Kareem that Slim was dead. What was shocking was that Frank was telling him that Kevin was the one who killed him. *This nigga just told me he killed Slim,* Mike thought to himself. He also heard Frank tell Kareem that Kevin killed Katrina. Lastly, he told Kareem that he killed Kevin in revenge. It confirmed that Frank was lying. Now the question was, why?

Frank didn't stay on the phone long. When Mike heard him hang up, he also heard screeching from the bed. By the time Frank walked into the kitchen, Mike was back at the table munching on his now soggy, Frosted Flakes.

"I gotta make a run, I'll be back," he told Mike.

"Where you headed?"

"Man, you asking too many questions, nigga. Just stay your ass here until I get back."

Mike stayed by the window until Frank drove off. He then grabbed his phone and tried calling Jessica. Maybe she knew more than him.

She picked up on the first ring.

"Hello?"

"Aye, Jess, this Mike. I'm calling about Kevin. I don't want to believe this shit I just heard. Please tell me he's alright."

"What did you hear?"

"I heard he was dead."

"And who did you hear that from?"

Mike hesitated but gave her the answer. "Frank told me." Jessica paused for a moment. "You still here?" Mike asked.

"Yeah, I'm here," she finally said. "No, Kevin is not dead, but he is barely hanging on to his life. Funny how Frank thinks he is, though. I wonder what he knows."

Mike let out a sigh of relief. "Damn, Jess. I hate that he got shot but glad to know he's alive."

"Well, I need answers, Mike. Why is Frank going around saying he's dead? What does he know?"

Mike slapped his forehead. He didn't want to tell her anything, but since Frank wasn't being truthful, he felt that he should at least say something. "Jess, keep this between you and I, but he might be the one who did it. He was just on the phone with this dude named Kareem and that's what he told him."

"But why?" Jessica cried. "Now, you see why I didn't trust y'all."

"Yeah, but listen, I'on know what the fuck Frank on right now."

"Well someone needs to know," she cried. "Two people are dead and one barely hanging on."

Mike eyes went round. "Yeah, I knew she wasn't coming out alive," he said, referring to Katrina. "I'm sorry—I tried to stop him, but he probably woulda shot me last night had I not left. His beef with her seemed personal."

"I'm going to the police," Jessica blurted out. "They need to stop him before he kills anyone else."

"No, don't do that, Jess. Let me see what's really going on first. I'ma call you in a few."

Mike felt the vibrations of someone walking on the old, wooden floors. He opened the curtain and saw Frank's car parked outside. He never even heard him come back in the house.

He quickly hung up the phone and opened his room door. As soon as he took the first step into the hallway, Frank came into view. He held the gun up at him and Mike trembled. He dropped his phone in the process.

"You headed somewhere?" Frank asked as he held a tight grip on his pistol. He loved seeing fear in others. He'd been that way since his youth.

Mike lifted his hands and stepped back. Frank followed him step by step and now they were back into Mike's room.

"Frank, what the fuck are you doing?" Mike said as he was being pushed onto his bed.

"Something I probably shoulda done a long time ago. You getting too soft, Mike. You just told that bitch everything."

"Look man, I didn't know what to think. You had just told me that Slim shot Kevin and you shot Slim in retaliation, but I heard you tell Kareem some other shit. That shit just sounds suspect."

"Suspect? Nigga, what's suspect is running your mouth to someone you barely know. That's Kevin's friend so you know her ass is going straight to the feds."

"No, she's not, bruh. I told her not to."

"She is." Frank's head nodded in a slow motion as he was thinking. "Now, you gonna make me have to kill the bitch."

"Kill her? We don't even get down like that, Frank. What the hell has gotten into you? And which story is the truth? The one you told me or told Kareem?"

Frank paced back and forth and tapped on his head, trying to think of his next move. Finally, he sat down across from Mike on a chair.

"You wanna know the truth, Mike? I shot Kevin."

Mike's forehead furrowed. "What did Kevin do to you for you to do him like that?"

"Money and power. I knew he didn't have the heart to cap Slim and Katrina so my plan was to kill them and his ass—but from what I heard in your conversation, Kev is still alive. I gotta finish him off."

"Man, Kev is cool as fuck. You ain't gotta do all that."

"Yeah, I do," he motioned. "I can't risk him talking to the cops or no one else. I need Antonio to know that I killed Slim and Katrina so I can collect the money that he was going to give to him. And I need Kareem to think Kevin killed Slim and Katrina so I can gain his trust back. Kareem and I are about to go into business."

"Damn, Frank," Mike said as he shook his head. "Man, I've been getting money with you since day one, but this shit ain't cool."

"That's how it is in the streets, Mike…And to be honest, my beef with Slim and Katrina was personal. She's the one who killed my uncle."

"Who Rodney?"

"Yep. I know it was her because she had on my grandma's necklace. Slim used to sell dope to Rodney so he's probably the one who set the shit up."

Mike understood where Frank was coming from since Rodney was more like a father to him—to both of them actually. Rodney always made sure they were good.

"So, what's up with Kareem?" Mike asked. "We've been beefing with this nigga for a minute. How you expect to do business with him?"

"Mike, like I said, I got this shit planned," he explained. "Kareem probably trusts me now so I'ma move a lil weight with him and we're gonna eventually take over Antonio's territory. Antonio won't see it coming because he gonna think I'm loyal to him since I killed Slim and Katrina."

"That shit ain't gonna work," Mike said to him. "Kareem and Antonio are enemies."

"Exactly. That's why I need Jessica and Kevin dead. Period. They're the only two besides you who know I shot him. I'ma find out what hospital he's at and finish his ass off. I need you go to Jessica's crib tonight and smoke that bitch."

"Nah, I can't do that, Frank. Look, me and Quentin really 'bout to get on this music shit as soon as he gets back from Oakland. I can't have a murder on my hands. Especially not from no shit like this. Jessica and Kev, ain't done nothing to nobody. You want this shit done, you gotta do it yourself."

"Oh, so, that's how it is?"

"Sorry, man but yeah."

Frank walked out of the room. Mike grabbed his phone to text Jess. He didn't want to snitch on Frank again, but he did want to warn her to leave town and have the hospital put security on Kevin.

Before he could send the text, Frank reappeared. He stood at the door, and raised the gun up at him. Mike's eyes went round and fear shot up to his chest. Without hesitation, Frank squeezed the trigger and the bullet pierced Mike's left shoulder.

Mike hollered in pain, and fell to the ground, clutching his wound. "We supposed to be homeboys," he let out.

Frank towered over him and showed no remorse. After hearing Mike's pleas, he grinned. "Nah, Mike. We WERE homeboys." He pressed the gun onto Mike's head and fired again.

Frank closed his eyes for a second to hold back a few tears. After that, he took a few valuables and left out. He knew he could never return.

CHAPTER THREE

We Need Answers

After getting off the phone with Mike, Jessica called the hospital to see if she could get an update on Kevin. All they were able to tell her was that he was in stable condition. Once she hung up with them, she broke the news to Nia, and she suggested that they drive up there. That way they could probably give them a more detailed update on him.

During the drive, Nia took in the breeze and the sights of the congested Los Angeles streets. She normally complained about the traffic, but strangely, she missed it. Matter of fact, she missed everything about L.A.

Once they arrived at the hospital, they went over to the front desk. Jessica had already spoken to the woman and felt that she had an attitude, so Nia went over and spoke to her.

"Hi, I'm here for an update on Kevin Dawson."

The woman's shoulders relaxed abruptly. She slammed her pen down. "One moment," she sighed as her stern face focused in on the monitor. "Wait. Didn't you just call?"

"Well, my friend did," Nia explained. "We decided to come up here in person, hoping to get a better update."

The woman shook her head and shrugged. "Well, ma'am I'm sorry, but I'm going to tell you the same thing I told her over the phone. He's stable but I am not allowed to release any more information unless you're kin to him."

"Well, I'm his ex," Nia replied, matching the woman's attitude. "He's been here since last night—we should be able to know something."

"What's your name and number? I'll have a nurse contact you."

"Nia. Nia Franklin. And I'm going to give you my address too. I am from out of town and will have to go back soon. Please give him all my information if you can."

The nurse forced out a counterfeit smile as she took Nia's information down. "Will that be all, Ms. Franklin?"

Nia turned and walked away.

"Anything?" Jessica asked as Nia approached her.

Nia sat next to her. "Nope. Maybe he's worse than we think."

"Or he could be trying to lay low."

"What do you mean?"

"Mike said that he believes Frank did it. I tried to get more information but the phone hung up suddenly. Kevin may know it was Frank and just requested that no one came and saw him."

"Well, I think we should tell this to the police."

*****

By the time they got back to Jessica's place, the sun had settled and the night sky took over. They both were beat. Jessica offered up her king-sized bed to Nia while she slept on the sofa. It was the least she could do for her— knowing that she had been up for nearly a full day.

Nia was almost asleep until her phone rang. She hopped up, hoping that it was the hospital calling.

"Oh ma' Gawd," she whined, just before drilling her head into the pillow. It was Greg. She hit the reject button and tossed her phone on the other side of the bed. She was stressed out enough and Greg would only add to it.

She missed being with Kevin. She wished she would've done more to get him away from the streets. They had a long history together and she felt she threw it away too quickly.

She began to think about how they first met. Nia was from the DFW area and moved to Jacksonville, Florida during her junior year of high school. She hated it at first because she had to leave her friends in Irving. That all changed once she met Kevin. Their love grew for each other in no time.

Even during the times that she and Greg were doing well, she thought about Kevin. She even got upset when she heard from Jess that Kevin had moved on and found someone else.

Nia sank in her thoughts and eventually drifted to sleep, but the sun crept in and woke her up a couple hours later. She could've fought it and went back to sleep, but with her buzzing phone, she gave in and woke herself up. She rolled over to the other side and grabbed it. Twenty-one missed calls and thirty-four text messages. The texts started off gentle and apologetic, but then went down the road of disrespectful and threatening.

She still didn't respond. She got out of bed and tiptoed to the kitchen, hoping to not disturb Jess. She grabbed a bottle of water from the fridge, and just as she was chugging it, she heard a sound coming from the living room.

"Hey," Nia said to Jess. "Did you get any sleep last night?"

Jessica sat her phone down and opened her mouth for a long yawn. "I slept for maybe two hours. I just got so much on my mind right now."

Jessica sat up to make room for her to sit down. Nia then took a sip of the water and placed it on the coffee table. "Yeah, I got a lot on my mind too, sis. I had to cut my phone off because Greg wouldn't stop calling me. That boy is a mess. I'm so done with his ass."

"So, Greg is that bad, huh?"

"Yass, chile. Greg is a little insecure boy pretending to be a man. If I wasn't so busy trying to free my mind from Kevin, I would've been realized it. All he's done is make me miss Kevin even more."

"Maybe after this is all over, you and Kevin can talk about your future again. I don't want to sound like I'm getting ahead of things, but I know you still love him and I bet he still loves you."

"Yeah, but that'll be a while from now. I'm sure he's mourning over her."

Jessica's phone rang during their conversation. She answered it and walked into her room. She was gone for about five minutes, and when she came back, she had on some different clothes.

"That was Detective Caldwell. He wants us to meet him at the hospital."

Nia had a rush of anxiety flow through her chest. "Did he say why?"

"No, he didn't."

Nia trotted to the room, and quickly unzipped her suitcase. She picked the first shirt and pants she laid eyes on, and quickly got into them.

They left in a hurry. Traffic was light on the Long Beach Freeway, but every unnecessary brake light and lane change pushed her adrenaline. She swerved through traffic and got there about five minutes faster than normal.

She opted for valet, versus searching for a spot in the garage. They exited the car in a hurry and headed to the door.

"Ms. Jones." The voice snatched her train of thought and her head swung in that direction.

"This way," she instructed Nia as they walked towards the man. "That's the detective."

His face didn't have bad news written on it, but that didn't stop her from questioning him. "Is Kevin okay?" Jessica asked. "Can we see him?"

"Kevin, is fine," he returned, but with a pause. "Or at least we believe so."

Jessica and Nia stared at each other, then Nia spoke. "What do you mean?"

Caldwell's shiny forehead creased. "And you are?"

"Nia Franklin. Kevin's ex."

"She's with me," Jessica added.

Caldwell took a deep breath before saying, "Come have a seat." He extended his hands to a vacant waiting area.

He shut the door behind him. He sat next to them and crossed his legs. Nia couldn't help but notice the tattoos and gold watch he had on. He didn't quite fit the detective type.

He cleared his throat, causing Nia to snap out of her observation. "Kevin left the hospital this morning on his own," he said, probing their reactions.

"How and when?" Jessica interrogated. "There's no way he could leave on his own power. Did you see him the other night?"

"I did. And I tried to question him about what happened, but he was highly sedated."

"Well, how can he go from that to leaving on his own?"

"His injuries weren't as severe as the doctors initially thought. He had on a vest that night and Jess when you found him unresponsive, he may have just blacked out from the fall or initial shock."

"I saw actual blood and wounds, though. It looked really bad."

"I understand," he nodded. "He does have a couple that did penetrate, and that's why the doctors and myself advise that he needs to come back. We believe he left because of a recent threat, but if I can contact him, I will assure him we have secured the building now."

"What kind of threat?" Nia asked.

"Yesterday the hospital received several calls from an unknown male asking what room Kevin was in. He wouldn't give them a name. Then, late last night a man was caught wandering the halls. One of the local authorities informed Kevin that he may be in danger, but by the time I got up here this morning, Kevin was gone."

"So, he could still be in danger, then," Nia added. "Is anyone out trying to find him?"

"Unfortunately, no. Kevin is not a suspect and since security cameras show him walking out and getting into a vehicle on his own, we have no reason to believe he left unwillingly. However, we do need to locate the man who was seen wandering. He drove a silver Lexus but the plates weren't registered."

"I think I know who it is," Jessica said while scrolling down on her phone. "A friend of Kevin's named Mike told me that this other guy named Frank shot him. I'm going to call him now."

Jessica called and the phone went straight to voicemail. Caldwell reached into his pocket a pulled out a note.

"Are you referring to Michael Reed and Franklin Armstrong?"

"I don't know their last names."

Caldwell smiled but quickly inversed. "Sorry for the smirk," he said to them. "It's just I believe I finally found the link. We were starting to believe that Nate may have shot Kevin, and then someone killed him and Katrina in retaliation...But then we asked, why would they kill Katrina? We almost believed that she may have been in on the attempt to murder Kevin, but after seeing text messages, we concluded that Kevin and Katrina were about to escape to Atlanta just hours before her murder."

Jessica nodded. "Yes, Katrina was innocent. She called me when Mike was at her house. She was supposed to be meeting me at Kevin's studio but that's when I found him and got a call from you saying Katrina was dead."

"Yes, so here's where we are. We searched the entire area of Kevin's studio. Not only was Slim, excuse me, Nate, found two hundred yards away, but we also found Henry Johnson's body. I've met Katrina, Slim, Henry and his deceased cousin, Chris, years ago so I knew a few of their mutual friends. The first two that I checked were, *Frank and Mike.* Upon entering the home, we found Mike deceased. Frank has not been located."

"Y'all need to find him," Jessica trembled. The thought of Frank being on the room shot fear in her. "Nia and I will try are best to look for Kevin."

"Just be careful," he said while rising from the chair. "If Frank shot the four of them, it's possible there could be more victims."

"I know."

"Have you two heard the name, Antonio Rivera?"

"Yeah, we have," Jessica responded. "He was the first person to get Kevin involved in this mess."

39

"What mess?"

Jessica shook her head quickly, hoping Caldwell would ignore her last statement. "Nothing. Kevin was just focusing on music and hung around the wrong people. He wasn't into whatever they were doing."

"Coo," he responded. "Yeah, Kevin had no priors. Seems to be a good kid. I'm interested in finding Antonio as well. Front what I hear, he's a big supplier in the streets. Maybe I will take all his money and go buy me an island somewhere," Caldwell joked.

"Then you will be as bad as the rest of them," Jessica returned. "Anyways, we really should get going. Nia is from out of town and will be leaving soon."

"Certainly," Caldwell said as they were walking out. "And one more thing…Unless someone on the outside spoke to Kevin already, he probably doesn't have a clue what happened to his fiancé."

CHAPTER FOUR

Back in Atlanta

After Nia got off work, she sat in her favorite restaurant for a few hours. She wasn't ready to go home and deal with Greg's shit. He'd already questioned her the entire week she'd been back.

Two hours and three glasses of wine later, she finally called it a night. She drove from the Dunwoody restaurant to their home in Woodstock. As soon as she arrived, she was met at the door.

"Oh, so you finally decided to come home?" he roared.

She ducked between his leaning arm, and squeezed herself through the tiny space between his large body and the doorframe. "Don't start with me today," she warned.

The door slammed shut, causing their picture to slide off one of its nails. Instead of fixing it, she took it off completely and set it on the entertainment center.

He followed her to the room. "Nia, the fuck is your problem?" he roared. "Why can't I get a word out of you anymore?"

Nia had given her all to Greg in the beginning and now there wasn't anything left. "You are my problem," she struck back. "I'm sick of your shit! What kind of man talks to his woman like that? All you do is run around accusing me of shit. You never stop and think about how I feel inside. I can't take this no more. I'm done with you."

Nia wanted to pull back her last statement, but seeing how calm Greg was at the moment, she held onto it. It wasn't that she didn't feel that way, she just didn't want to get pushed down or grabbed.

"Nia, I'm sorry," a coughing and teary eyed Greg responded. "Look, I know my behavior has been worse, but it's because—"

Greg's coughing wouldn't let him get his words out. Nia stormed passed him, bumping into him on her way out. "There ain't no excuse to treat someone like that, Greg."

Nia sat on the couch. Greg did what he normally did after an argument—He locked himself into the guest room. He knew Nia hated when he drank liquor; so he stashed bottles in there and drank until he gets tore up or until Nia gives in and talk to him…But not this time. Nia was through. She knew she had to think of somewhere to go. It wouldn't happen overnight, though.

The wine she had earlier set her off into a deep sleep.

*****

Nia woke up at 7:15 the next morning. Having to be at her job in Dunwoody by eight, she decided to not even rush. 575 was probably a parking lot, and I-75 and 285 wouldn't be any better.

She checked her phone. Two texts from Greg.

Gone to Chicago

Be back in a couple days

The concern wouldn't get to her this time. A simple, "ok," would even be too much. Greg always pulled stunts like this. A couple months prior he told her he was going to L.A., but she found him drunk at a hotel in Kennesaw. She sat her phone down and went to the room to shower.

After her shower, she heard a knock at the door. The knock was firm, drawing in concern. Outside of a few neighbors, they never had unannounced visitors; and definitely not at seven in the morning.

"Who is it?" she asked, pulling up the towel to cover her breasts. She wasn't going to open the door with her body exposed, but she at least wanted to see who it was.

"Me."

The voice was muffled yet deep.

"Greg?" she assumed. "Where is your key?"

She focused in on the glazing door. The man said something else, but she was too focused in on his appearance. Almost tall enough to be Greg, but the weight of the person seized that thought away from her.

"Just wait a second," Nia said. She went back to the room and picked up a pair of shorts and a tee from the floor. She slipped it on and went back up to the front.

"Who you say you were again?" This time she asked while being closer to the door.

"Me, Nia. Kevin."

Kevin, she said to herself. *No way.* She unlatched the deadbolt and turned the knob. The first thing she saw was a dingy man standing in front of her.

"Nia," he said, surprised to see her.

His breath stung her nose.

She held her breath for a moment as she studied him. Once familiarity struck, her frown lifted into a smile.

"Oh my God, Kevin! You look so different," she said, referring to his low haircut and muscle gain. "How did you get here?"

She pulled him in and hugged him. It was obvious that he hadn't bathe in days—maybe years with the way he smelled. She kept a smile and just held her breath as much as she could.

He shrugged. "It's a long story, Nia. I got out of there as quick as I could."

The wind slammed on her face. "It's chilly out here. Come in."

She knew she had to be careful since Greg went to *Chicago,* but she still invited him in. He limped over to the chair she pulled out for him and noticed the walking boot on his right foot.

"Nia, you just don't know how happy I am to see you right now," he said to her. "I thought about you a lot during all this mess."

"I'm just glad you're alright, Kevin. You had me and Jessica worried. The detective told us that you left the hospital."

"Yeah, because I kept getting threatening phone calls so I called one of my homeboys to come get me. His wife is actually an R.N. at that same hospital, so she was able to get me free meds, this damn walking boot and some other shit. And she got your name and number from the receptionist and gave it to me. Once I was good enough to stand on my own, I got my ass on the bus and came here. I wanted to call you, but since you left your address, I figured I would just come see you. I missed you, Nia. You just don't know how good I felt when I found out you came to check on me."

Nia was saddened by his health, but she smiled knowing he was here with her.

"So, you must've not let Jessica know you're okay. We said we would call each other if we heard from you."

Kevin smacked his teeth. "Man, fuck Jessica. Fuck Katrina. Fuck Slim. And everybody else. I'm putting all that shit behind me."

Nia's mouth dropped. She then remember last week when the detective stated that Kevin may not know about Katrina being murdered. She came up with a way to see if he did or not.

"Did you even talk to Katrina or Jess? Why are you saying that about them?"

46

"Nope, and I don't plan to, either. Jess was supposed to pick me up but she never came...And Katrina probably was setting me up all along. I ain't heard from her and she didn't come see me at the hospital."

Maybe it was the medication or the slight smell of alcohol on his breath, but she knew he wasn't in the right state of mind.

"Kevin, Jessica is the one who found you laying in the street. Had she not gotten there in time, you may have bled to death. She called me that same night and told me what happened. I went straight to the airport and bought a ticket for the next flight to L.A. Jess and I searched everywhere for you during the three days I was there."

"Look, I'm not saying she had something to do with it, but I don't know. What if someone scared her off and she was just scared to warn me? Regardless of what happened, I know L.A. ain't safe for me. I still don't know who shot me."

"Did you talk to the police or that detective?"

"Nope. Not since I saw them at the hospital. They tried questioning me but I was too high off all that damn medicine they gave me."

"Frank shot you," Nia said abruptly.

"Frank?" Kevin smirked. "Nah, Frank and I were cool. If anything, Slim set this shit up…And between me and you, Nia, I should have shot that nigga when I had the chance."

"Kevin, Slim and Katrina are—" Nia stopped midsentence. With Kevin already delusional, there was no way she would let him know now. She would eventually think of a way, but it would have to wait.

"Slim and Katrina, what?" he asked. "Don't say they're innocent too."

She shook her head and replied, "Nothing, Kevin. Listen, we need to get you cleaned up."

Nia walked to Greg's closet and pulled out the Polo outfit that she bought him for his birthday. It was a size too small, and she never bothered to exchange it. Luckily Greg had an unopened pack of boxers as well. She ripped the packaging off, pulled out a pair and sat it next to the outfit.

Kevin limped his way to her room without her knowledge. His eyes scanned the entire room.

"Yeah, I forgot you got a man, now," he said with his head lowered. "At least tell him thanks for the clothes."

She smirked at his sarcasm. "Kevin, if you only knew."

His arms extended. "What?"

"Nothing. Come on, let's get you in the shower. I have an important meeting at work today."

She helped him shower and get dressed. Greg still hadn't come home. She threw Kevin's old clothes away and they both got into her car.

"I'm going to get you a hotel by my job. I'll come see you when I get off. You shouldn't have to go anywhere because there's plenty of restaurants nearby that do delivery."

"I'll probably settle for something in the vending machine. I don't have much on me."

"I got you," she said. "Remind me when we get to the hotel."

"Nia I can't," he sighed. "You've already done enough."

"Kevin, don't tell me how to handle MY money," she said with a playful frown. "If I want to give you some money then I can. You know darn well you can't survive off chips all day."

"You're right," he chuckled. "I just feel like I've let you down so many times and no matter what, you always seem to be there for me."

Nia didn't respond. She just took a moment to enjoy Kevin's appreciation of her.

After getting past the usual Atlanta congestion, they arrived at the hotel. Nia had less than ten minutes to spare. Luckily her job was just a traffic light away, but she still had to get him upstairs.

"Alright, Kevin, I will see you later," she said while heading for the door. "I'll be back by four, but make sure you call me if you hurt yourself or something. The money is on the table."

"Yes ma'am," he joked.

As soon as she looked at Kevin again she almost cried. She missed him more than she ever had and she thanked God silently for keeping him alive.

"Nia wait," Kevin said to her. He pushed his injured foot off the bed first then pulled his body up. He slid to her as quick as he good.

"Nia, you may not believe me, but I thought about you a lot. I think destiny has its way of happening no matter what."

"Maybe so."

They stared at each other. Nia then closed her eyes and moved her face towards his. As soon as their lips connected, she trembled and tears followed. Not just tears from the joy of having Kevin right next to her again, but the guilt of knowing his fiancé was dead and he had no knowledge of it.

*****

Nia couldn't focus in the meeting. The latte with the extra shot of espresso she got from her job's café, had her jittery. Or maybe it was still the unsettled guilt they flowed through her.

I gotta call Jess.

After the meeting, she closed her office door and settled in her seat. She took out her phone and called Jess.

"Hey, Nia! How you doing?" Jessica shouted on the other end.

The cheerfulness seemed awkward to her. "What you so happy about, girl?"

"I just got offered a position in New York! K.P. is expanding his label and wants me as the in-house engineer there. It's a dream come true!"

"Good," Nia replied in a muted tone.

"You're okay, Nia?"

"Kevin's here," she said, plain and dry.

"Are you serious? That's good news, girl! We can finally stop being so paranoid and I now can celebrate my new position with K.P."

"Yeah, that part is good," Nia replied. "But he came here without talking to anyone in Cali about anything. He still doesn't know that Katrina's dead."

"Oh my God, how are you gonna tell him?"

"I don't know, Jess. He was saying bad stuff about her, and I wanted to tell him then, but couldn't."

"I understand, girl. That's gonna be hard to do alone. Where is he now?"

"I got him a hotel down the street from my job. I'ma just keep him there until I figure out what my next move gonna be. Greg and I are breaking up."

"See, that's a sign, girl. You were already having problems with Greg and now Kevin shows up. You two gonna be good. I tell you what, call me when you get next to him. Maybe we can tell him together."

"I don't know, Jess. It's kinda complicated."

"No, what's going to be complicated if he finds out from someone else and then finds out that you knew all along."

"Not that," Nia replied. "It's Kevin. He went on a rant about you and everyone else down there. I think it's the medicine, though. He said he didn't want to talk to anyone there. He'll come through I'm sure."

"Wait, wait," Jessica said as her tone changed. "What do you mean about going on a rant about me?"

"He just said everyone down there probably played a role in him getting shot—But please, don't take it personal, Jess. I'ma let him rest today and maybe try tomorrow."

"You gotta be shitting me," Jess ranted. "So, he brought his ass all the way from Cali to Georgia to see you, but couldn't call me because he think I had something to do with it?"

Nia felt the need to defend him. "He's just scared. We don't know what it's like to be shot, Jess. Can you at least understand before getting upset?"

"Whatever, Nia. I may not know what it's like to be shot, but I've always been there for Kevin. When you left him the first time, guess who was there? Me. I was there when he thought Katrina was shady—I helped him with school and everything. If he wanna turn his back on me then fuck it. He's done, I'm done. "

Realizing the call went south, Nia tried to clear the air. "Jess, I'm sorry. It's just everything caught me by surprise. You gotta understand where I'm coming from."

"Look Nia, I'm done. I am about to move to New York and be happy for myself for a change. And you more than anyone should know I wouldn't do something like that. We stayed up for two nights looking for him."

"I know, and I told him that."

"Bye, Nia."

"Wait...How am I supposed to tell him about Katrina?"

"Girl, that's your problem. And if he runs his ass back here looking for answers, please don't call me."

CHAPTER FIVE

Payday

It was too late to turn back. Frank murdered his best friend and was now on his own. Despite the slight feeling of grief, he couldn't let it stop his paper chase.

His unsuccessful attempt to kill Kevin, stalled his plans—just for a moment, though. He didn't want to go pay Antonio or Kevin a visit just yet, just in case Kevin ran his mouth.

He crashed at a hotel fifty miles outside of the city for a few days. He still had the small bag of money he took from Kevin when he shot him, but he was ready for more. On the third day, he called a mutual friend of theirs by the name of Quentin. Frank knew Quentin because he used to slang with him back in the day, but now was one of Mike's rappers. Quentin was back and forth living in Oakland with his girl but also L.A. with his other family.

Frank knew he hadn't been back to L.A. for a minute.

"Yo, Q, how you, bruh?" Frank greeted when he answered.

"What up, Frank. I was just about to call your ass. I been trying to reach Mike. I got a new track I want him to hear."

"Man, I-ain' heard from Mike in a few days myself," Frank lied. "I've been out of town on business."

"True that."

"Aye you seen Kev?" Frank asked. "I got a nigga I know who wanna buy some beats from him."

"Damn, you ain't heard what happened?" Quentin stated. "Kev got shot about a week ago."

"Whaaaat," Frank said, horribly. "Nah, I didn't hear. Where he at now?"

"Man, that nigga left and went to Atlanta. He said he ain't coming back."

"Who told you that?"

"My partner who I used to get beats from named Zay. Zay moved to Atlanta about five years ago. He said Kevin called him two days ago and told him he was on a bus to Atlanta because he got shot and was trying to get away."

"Do he know who did it?"

"Nope. That's probably why he left. Kevin can make some hard ass beats but you know he ain' got no gangsta in him."

"Alright, Q," Frank said to him. "If Mike call me, I'ma tell him to holla at you."

"Bet, cuz."

All Frank had to do now was go tell Antonio that he did what Kevin was supposed to do. If the plan went the right way, he expected Antonio to pay him what he offered Kevin.

He decided to call up one of Antonio's men, Felipe. Frank met him back in the day with Chris. Felipe was Antonio's right-hand man. He did anything Antonio asked of him. No job was too big or too small for him. Whether it be blowing the brains out of an enemy, or taking one of Antonio's kids to school, he got it done.

"Felipe, this Frank. I need to holla at Antonio."

"Tonio is out of the country," he replied, with his heavy, Spanish accent.

"Coo. Listen, I got some news for him that will make him real happy. Slim and Katrina are taken care of."

"Awesome," Felipe said. We heard about it in the streets, but Kevin never showed up to collect his pay."

Ron Leath

"That's because Kevin ain't have the heart to do it. I did it. Let Antonio know I got him with whatever he needs."

"I'm sure he'll be pleased. Keep your line open. I will contact you when he's back in town."

*****

Frank continued to stay ducked off until he got the call from Antonio. He then made his way back to the city to meet him. When he got there, Antonio, along with Felipe and a few others were already there waiting on him. They patted him down and released him once they didn't find any weapons.

Antonio took him to his office. "So, Felipe tells me you took care of my problem. I must say I'm surprised. Slim was one of your friends."

"Yeah, *was*," Frank replied. "Slim had it coming for a long ass time. He killed Chris."

"Yes, I know…But Frank, I never saw you as a killer. What made you kill that beautiful sister of his as well?"

"That bitch killed my uncle years ago. If I had more time, I would've made that bitch suffer."

Antonio loved to see a man that didn't show fear and did what they had to do. He patted Frank on the back. "I knew right when Kevin left my club that he wouldn't do it. If he's in Atlanta, he better stay his ass in Atlanta."

"Kevin wasn't built for this shit. No disrespect to Chris, but I don't know what he saw in Kevin."

Antonio lifted his chin and moved his hands around his ashy, grey beard. He studied Frank. As far as he knew, Frank was being honest about everything.

"Well, I guess it's only right that I give to you, what I promised him."

Antonio extended his hand towards a cabinet that was towards the back of the room. One of his men opened it and pulled out a bag and walked it over to Frank.

"Open it," Antonio said to him.

Frank unzipped the bag. A bundle of hundred-dollar bills spilled out. "Damn, this for me?"

Antonio nodded. "Yes. Frank, I want you on my team. I have a big shipment coming in shortly that's going to put us over the top. I will be getting the keys at a very low price. Until then, I want you to move a lil weight around for me. I'll get my men to contact you. Maybe you can work your way up like Chris did."

Frank smiled. "Whatever you need, I got you."

"Listen, if Kevin ever decides to come back here, he's a dead man."

"No doubt," Frank agreed. "I'll kill him myself."

Antonio walked Frank out of the club. The meet up was short and simple, just like Frank wanted it. He gained Antonio's trust quicker than he thought he would. He knew in no time he would be able to take over.

As he walked to his car, Felipe came running out behind him. "Frank wait a sec," he said as he caught up to him. "I want to have a word with you."

"Sure, sup?"

"Walk this way."

Felipe lead him to a dark area far from the door. His eyes stared down Frank's throat. Frank tensed slightly, as this caught him off guard.

"Everything good?" he asked Felipe.

Felipe tilted his head to the left. "I don't know, Frank. Antonio doesn't know a lot about what goes on out here so I have to be his eyes sometimes. And I see bullshit all over you."

Felipe reached into his coat pocket. Frank's eyes widened as he slowly began to tremble. When Felipe's hand emerged, he simply had an envelope in his hand."

"What's this?" he asked, calming himself once he realized it wasn't a gun.

"Open it when you leave. If it's money and power you're after, then I can get you that. Follow my plan and we can take over and kill that son of a bitch Antonio."

CHAPTER SIX

All Good?

Nia made it to the room a quarter past four. She heard his snoring before she even opened the door. She walked in and saw him sound asleep.

He was awakened by the thud as the door closed.

"Sorry," she said to him in a whisper. "I didn't think it would slam like that."

She hoped that he would go back to sleep—to give her time to think, but Kevin crawled off the bed and went to the restroom. When he came back, he sat at the table with her.

"How was work?"

"Fine."

"What's wrong? Did something happen?"

Nia rose her chest and let it slowly flow down with a light exhale. "Kevin, I have to tell you something."

"Let me guess, you regret that kiss you gave me earlier?" he joked.

"No, Kevin," she said as she placed her fingers on her forehead. "I have something to tell you that may change everything."

Kevin's concern drew in. He reached over and held her hand. "Nia, just tell me. I'm sure we can handle it together."

"She's dead."

Kevin leaned his body back and released his hand from her quickly. "Who?"

Tears fell down her face. "Katrina. She died the same night you were killed."

"What?" Her response caused his heart rate to increase rapidly. "Nia, what are you talking about? Are you sure? How do you know Katrina?"

"The detective told us. He said he tried to tell you but you left the hospital before he had the chance. Kevin, I'm so sorry I didn't tell you earlier."

Nia began to cry uncontrollably. Kevin started with sniffles before going into a full breakdown. He still felt the need to comfort Nia.

"It's not your fault, Nia," he said while shaking his head. "This is on me. I should've never fucking left without knowing the truth. I have to go back."

"And do what, Kevin? You're not healthy enough to go after someone."

"A bullet don't need arms and feet, Nia. I'ma find out who did this shit."

Kevin became angrier as he thought about it. His eyes were fiery red.

The worst was happening. Nia didn't know what to say or do. She tried rubbing his arms, hoping it would calm him. "Frank is behind all of this, Kevin. Please let the detective do his job."

"It gotta be deeper than that. Frank's not a killer, Nia. Antonio is responsible for this shit. Katrina and I were supposed to start a life together and away from all the bullshit. He gotta pay."

"Baby, Antonio is a drug lord," Nia pleaded with compassion. "How can you expect to get to him?"

"I'll find away. Even if it kills me to do so."

"So, what about me?" she asked, trying to hold her head straight. The wobbling fear made her shake.

Kevin was ready to go. Nia's desperation caused him to shift some of his anger towards her. He stood to put his clothes on.

"Nia, you made your choice by leaving me before. Had I not got shot in the first place, you wouldn't have even reached out to me. Go be with that cop dude."

"Kevin, why are you saying this to me?" she cried. "Leaving you was the hardest thing I've ever done. I don't love him. I love you."

Kevin shook his head as he released fast and heavy breaths. "That ain't my problem, Nia. Frank, Antonio or whoever, killed the woman I love. Nothing else matters."

After getting his clothes on, he headed for the door. She tried one last chance to prove her loyalty and keep him safe. She hugged his body and wedged herself between the opened space in the door and the frame.

"Kevin, let me go with you then," she pleaded. I wouldn't be able to live with myself if something happened to you."

He shook his head. "Nia, I'm sorry, but this is my fight. I gotta avenge the murder of my fiancé."

He pulled away, forcing her into releasing her grip. Nia accidentally fell to the ground and clutched her knee.

Kevin stared at her compassionately, but after she appeared to be okay, he opened the door again and left.

CHAPTER SEVEN

Whispering Streets

Frank didn't expect the streets to be as quiet as they were. He thought for sure that the feds would be on to him by now. He jumped around from place to place until he was ready to call Kareem.

A week had passed since he last spoke to Kareem. He called him up anyway. "Yo, you ready to do business?" Frank asked.

"Business? Fuck is you talking about Frank?" Kareem replied.

"The same shit we spoke about last week. I'm in business with Antonio now. I'm ready to get paid. I know he's your competition, so I say we learn all his secrets and knock his head off. I got a nigga on the inside who gonna help us too."

"Man, I'on talk business on the phone," Kareem said to him. "Come by the crib this evening. I need to holla at you 'bout something anyway."

Kareem hung up. Frank had a few errands to run and once he was done, he headed over there. When he got there, Kareem's baby mama, Quelle, opened the door for him. She wore the same short shorts as always.

"Hey Frank, long time no see. Kareem in the back, playing spades."

He stared at her ass as he followed her to the back. He then found Kareem at the kitchen table smoking weed and playing cards.

"Sup, Kareem," Frank nodded.

Kareem looked up to acknowledge him, but then played his hand. Kareem was gangsta and always kept cool. Even if he was about to do something crazy, he always remained calm. Frank tried to go with the flow, but couldn't read him.

After Kareem played his hand, he got up from the table. "Go out back," he said to Frank. "I'ma be out there in a minute."

"A'ight cool," Frank nodded.

The other men remained seated at the table but their eyes followed Frank until he was out of their view.

Frank stepped out onto the deck then walked down the four steps. The dim light on the back of the house was the only light around. He heard the pits barking but could only see their glowing eyes. Suddenly, he heard footsteps behind him. When he turned around, Kareem was there, pointing the pistol at him.

He took a step back and raised his hands. "Whoa, Kareem. What the hell, cuz?"

Kareem cocked the pistol. "Frank your lil bullshit story ain't adding up. You called me and told me some buster named Kevin killed Slim. But why call me? You and I were beefing for years. Slim was your boy too. You could've smoked Kevin ya' damn self."

Frank tried to suppress his shivers. Being scared wasn't the best thing for him at that moment. He had to talk his way out of it.

"Look man, Kevin ain't a problem no more. I reached out to you for a business opportunity."

"Frank you so full of shit," Kareem laughed while shaking his head. "Nigga, word on the street is that a price was out on Slim and his sister. Next thing I know, I'm hearing that they're dead. And guess who told me first? Your bitch ass. You fucked with my folks and you 'bout to get cha' head knocked off."

Kareem slapped him upside his head with the pistol and kicked him in the leg. "Don't think I'on know about Mike, also. See, Frank, I sent some niggas after you. They got to your house and saw yellow tape everywhere. Some lil' bitch said that Mike got killed. You were nowhere to be found."

"I had to lay low," he said quickly. "Kevin probably got to Mike, too."

Kareem gave a half smile. "So, this *lil* nigga did all that, ha? How come I ain't never heard of him?"

"He was the dude running packages for Chris a while back."

Kareem lifted his chin. "You talking about the same nigga who Slim was looking for? The fuck nigga who was fucking around with his sister?"

"Yeah," Frank nodded. "He took the bag of money from Slim the same night Chris got killed. He shot Henry that night, too and killed Kandy."

Kareem drew in a deep breath. His other homies were standing on the porch now. "Y'all hear this nigga, right?" he said to them. "He must don't know I talked to Slim after that shit went down. Slim said Kevin was scared as fuck that night. Of course, he could overpower

Henry's lil weak ass and a girl, but when Slim went looking for that nigga again, he ran off like a bitch."

Frank was cornered. As they closed in on him, with their weapons drawn, he gave one last speech.

"Wait," he raised his hands to defend himself. I got five hundred racks that Antonio gave me for joining his crew. To prove my I'm serious about business, I'll split that shit with you."

"Hold my gun," Kareem said to one of his boys. "Stand up," he demanded Frank. As soon as he did, Kareem balled his fists and landed one on Frank's jaw. "Nigga, Antonio ain't giving you no muthafucking large amount just to join his team. This ain't no muthafucking Fortune 500 company with sign-on bonuses and shit. This a damn drug empire. And if you ask me, five hundred racks sound like a hit. A big one at that."

Kareem continued to pound Frank with his fists. Once he fell, his homeboys came over and stomped him. Kareem took the gun and held it to Frank's head.

"Slim was like a brother, nigga. And Katrina was my sister. You fucked with the wrong family."

"Wait," a distant voice shouted. Kareem held his head up and Toya emerged from the dark patio. "Kareem, he might be telling the truth," she huffed. "I just got off the phone with Kevin. He's headed back here from Atlanta."

"Toya, Kevin ain't do that shit. This fat fuck did."

"Kevin probably played a part too—at least with Katrina's death. She came to my house the night she was killed. She said her and Kevin almost shot each other, but he was able to convince her that he was innocent. He sent her to my house and told him to wait for her there. She waited over an hour, but got tired of waiting so she went to look for him. That was the last time I saw her alive."

Kareem looked at Frank. He was bruised up. "Get up," he said to him. Kareem was never the one to apologize, and especially not to him because he felt that he still had something to do with it, but since Toya mentioned Kevin, he decided to spare Frank for now.

"I want one of y'all to find him and bring him to me," Kareem said to Frank and Toya. "And Frank, I want him alive."

"I got ya."

"Oh, and yo' ass ain't off the hook yet, nigga. I find out you had something to do with this, I'ma kill yo ass without hesitation. And matter of fact, I want that whole five hunid you got. Have that shit to me within 24 hours or you better not ever bring your ass around here again."

CHAPTER EIGHT

A Bombshell

Nia stayed on the floor for about five minutes after Kevin left. She was angry at him for not seeming to care about her feelings, but her anger eventually subsided when she thought about the dangers Kevin was about to go back to.

She pulled herself up, and ran down to the lobby. After not seeing him there, she went outside. She screamed his name in every direction. The only person outside was a cab driver.

"Hello sir," she said as she approached him.

The driver was Asian. He looked up at her and smiled. "Hi, you need a ride?"

"No, I'm looking for my boy—I meant friend," she corrected. She raised her hand way above her head. "He's about this tall, baldhead and had on a red shirt with white pants."

"Yes, I saw him. He just hopped in the other cab. He was looking for a ride to the bus station, I think."

"Thank you."

Nia ran back upstairs to get her purse. She grabbed her phone and called him, but a woman answered.

"Hi, I'm looking for Kevin," she said.

"Kevin?" the woman replied. "You have the wrong number.

"Shit," she mumbled. "Sorry," she said before hanging up. She had Kevin's old number. She then tried to call Jess back.

"Nia, what now?" Jess answered.

"Jess, listen. I'm sorry about earlier today but I need Kevin's number."

Jess laughed. "Lemme guess, you told him about Katrina and he left, right. Sounds like Kevin to me."

"Look, this is serious," she argued. "I need to talk to him now. I don't have his new number."

"I'll text it to you in a minute. I'm driving back to the house now. And if he left while he was right there with you, you should know a phone call is not going to do any good."

"Well, that's my only option."

"Give me five minutes."

Nia sat on the bed and waited. Every possible scenario played in her head. If Frank didn't get him, maybe some of Slim's people thought he did it and would retaliate. Or even Antonio may be looking for him. She knew she had to find a way to stop him from going.

Her thoughts made the time fly by and when she looked at her watch, nearly thirty minutes had passed. Jess still hadn't sent her the text, but instead of bothering her again, she decided to go look for him herself. She drove to the downtown bus station and searched for him. She made eye contact with every person and even waited by the bathrooms. Kevin was nowhere to be found.

She finally went up to the counter and completely ignored that the employee was helping another customer. The customer saw how frantic she was so she stepped out of the way.

"When is the next bus to Los Angeles leaving?" she rushed.

The man looked at her then slowly turned away towards his screen; having not one bit of care about her behavior.

"Would you like to buy a ticket?"

She shook her head quickly. "No, I just need to know when the next one is leaving or if you can tell me if someone bought a ticket. I have a friend who's in danger and I need to stop him from getting on the bus."

"Ma'am, if someone is in danger we have an officer on site that can help you. I can't release passengers' names to you unless they're minors and you show proof of your relationship. Otherwise, see the officer over there."

The employee went back to helping the other customer and Nia stormed off. She stayed a while, but after no luck, she eventually left.

Jessica finally sent Kevin's number through text then called her.

"Did you get it?" she asked.

"I did, thanks."

"I meant to send it earlier, but I was heading to the store to get some paint. I found a renter for my house earlier than expected…And just so you know, I called Kevin but he didn't pick up for me earlier."

"Yeah, I stayed at the bus station for over an hour and he never showed up. I just hope he thinks about it before heading there."

"Nia, I think you're putting too much effort in this. I'm sorry for my attitude earlier, but you just don't know what Kevin has put me through. When you left him the first time, he went M.I.A. on me for a minute. Then he just wouldn't listen and kept chasing money. I really hope he's okay too, but at the end of the day, he has to make his own decisions."

"You're right, but I got a lot going on and this just adds to my stress. I guess I'll stay at the hotel that I got for him because Greg and I are through. I'm not going back to the house with him."

"I understand." she rushed. "And I hate to get off the phone so soon, but I need to paint this room tonight. I'm moving in three days to New York, so I have little time to get this place clean. If he calls or somehow ends up in Cali, I will tell him to call you."

"Okay, Jess. And that thank you again for giving me his number."

"Sure."

Nia called him but he still didn't answer. She tried again that night and his phone went straight to voicemail.

CHAPTER NINE

Jessica

Blessings were pouring in for Jessica. She was just hours away from moving to New York to work with K.P. fulltime. She had just got through shipping her important items and all she needed to do was a little touch up on the house. She had already repainted the walls, pressure washed the floors, but still felt she needed to do more.

Despite being happy about the move, she was going to miss living in the house. At the young age of seventeen, her mom passed away and left her the house. After her uncle died a couple years later, she had to find a way to pay the bills so she was forced to drop out of college and work full-time and the grocery store. She put in hard work and couple years later, she joined the Music Production School. And now it was about to all pay off.

The tenant was scheduled to come over at five that evening. She would do a quick walkthrough with them and head to the airport by eight for her late evening flight.

Around two, someone knocked at the door. "Uggh! Why are they here already?" she whined while looking at her watch. She hurried down the hall and opened the door.

"Kevin?" she confirmed.

"Jess, we need to talk."

"Yeah, we do," she said while opening the door to let him in. "Why did you come back? Nia's been calling me every hour for the last three days looking for you."

"I know," he said while looking around at the empty living room. He made his way to the mounted bar stools and sat. "Zay is in Atlanta too, so I stayed with him for a couple days. He shot me some bands and I flew up here. I only plan on being here a couple days to find answers, so I don't want to call her and have her worried."

"That's so selfish of you, Kevin. That girl stopped everything to come here and check up on you. Why do you keep turning your back on people who love you, but then come back when you need something?"

"None of this was planned, Jess. I went straight to Atlanta after getting out the hospital. I felt something immediately when I saw Nia, but when she told me about Katrina, I snapped."

"See, that's what I'm saying. You're playing with people's emotions. She is going crazy looking for you. Then look what you told her about me. You said you didn't want anything to do with anyone in Cali. And I hope like hell you weren't serious when you said I could been on it too."

"What?" he frowned.

"Umm hmm, Nia told me. That sounds like you. Always running away and wanna forget everyone."

"You're right and I'm sorry," he confessed. "I just really need a couple days to find answers. Can you call her and tell her I'm okay?"

"No, you call her. Tell her the truth."

"Maybe later," he sighed. "I need to stop a few places and ask some questions."

"You don't need to do that, Kevin," she said while going in her purse. "And here." She handed him two sets of keys. "These are to Katrina's condo and yours. The lady didn't want to give me hers, but I lied and said we were kin. Luckily are last names are both Jones. All I did was show her my license and she gave me the keys."

"Coo. Maybe I will stop by there today too. Grab a few things and take it back to Atlanta with me."

"Where you gonna stay in Atlanta?"

"Maybe with my boy, Zay. He got a bedroom at the studio and said I could stay anytime I needed to…But, if I ain't burn my bridge with Nia yet, I may see what we can do. She said she loves me and that she and that cop are done, so we'll see."

"That's why you need to go back, Kevin. I am not trying to sound funny, but Katrina is gone. Nia is here and loves you."

"I love her too. She was the first person I ran too after that shit happened. It's just I won't be able to live without answers. I need to know if it was personal or some shit that Antonio ordered."

"Kevin, I'm sure Nia and anyone else you talked to told you Frank did it. Let the cops handle it. They know it's him and are looking for him. I bet he's probably already left the area."

"If Frank did it and left town, then that only means one thing; Antonio paid him off. There's no way Frank killed all them just to leave town for nothing—unless he has a hidden motive."

"Wait," Jessica said, holding her finger up. "What's all this about Antonio giving away money? Nia mentioned that to me, too. How do you know? Did Antonio want them dead?"

Kevin held his head down and confessed. "Yeah, he initially wanted me to kill them."

"Why Kevin? What else were you involved in?"

"Nothing. I swear. It's just Frank and Mike came to me and said that Antonio wanted me to do a small job that would pay a lot. I agreed because I knew Katrina and I were moving to Atlanta, so I wanted to get any extra money I could. But when I went there, it wasn't what I expected. He told me the story about how Katrina and Slim were plotting to take me out, and said he would pay me half a million if I killed them. I knew I wasn't going to do it, but I had to tell him I would so I could get out alive...I'm guessing he sent Frank behind me."

Jessica shook her head. "Why didn't you and Katrina leave right then? Why were you at the studio and she was at her friend's house then her condo with Mike?"

"That's when all hell broke loose," he explained. "Katrina and I damn near killed each other thinking we were setting each other up. Her brother came over and talked to her while I was at Antonio's club. After we got that shit settled, I told her to meet me at Toya's in an hour, but I got kidnapped by Slim and Henry. When I called you was when I got free."

"Kevin, I hear you, but this is all the more reason you should leave. You will never know the truth because if you go confront one of them, they will kill you. Even if you don't confront them and continue to search for other things, they may find you. Go drop that rental back off and get on a plane."

He thought about it and sighed. "You know, you might be right. Maybe I'll just stop by the condo and see what I can find and after that, I'll probably head back."

"I hope you do, Kevin. Because you may find something that you don't like. Sometimes the truth is too much to handle…It doesn't always set you free. What if you discovered that she was really plotting to kill you, or that she may have been involved in something really deep? Would you be able to rest with that type of closure?"

"Probably not, Jess."

"Exactly, and I hate to cut this short, but I am trying to leave as soon as I give this man these keys. I got to finish up. Just call me sometime, Kev. I will see you around."

"Cool, I will."

She walked him out to the car and hugged him for about twenty seconds. Light tears rolled down her face but she wiped them before he saw them. She had a feeling Kevin would be hardheaded and continue to search for answers. She also knew that she had to stay out of it and let him decide his own life.

As he drove away, she let out a heavier cry, knowing that this was probably the last time she would see him. Not because he would get killed, but because she was moving to New York and putting everything else behind her.

CHAPTER TEN

Help from an Old Friend

"Nia," Jess said when she answered. "Did Kevin call you?"

"No, you heard from him?"

"Yeah, he stopped by the house a few hours ago. I told him to leave town but to call you first."

"Oh my God," Nia sighed. "Where is he now? What if he gotten himself in trouble?"

"I doubt it. He's probably somewhere around here looking for answers. I thought I talked some sense into him about going back to Atlanta. He told me he was going to stop by the condo first then head to the airport. Did you try calling him again?"

"Yes, several times but his damn phone is off. I don't know what else to do."

"That damn, Kevin," Jessica sighed. "Nia, I know you love him, but you gotta let him do him. Kevin is hardheaded. He was talking about going after Frank and Antonio, but I told him that's not smart. Those guys would kill him without question."

"So, any clue where he might be?"

"No, Nia. Sorry. I'm at the airport heading to New York. Otherwise, I would drive around looking for him."

"Should I call that detective?"

"You *can*...but I don't really trust him. What detective you know wears Gucci suits all the time and drives that type of car? And when he made that joke about taking all of Antonio's money, I kinda believe that's something he would do."

"Probably," Nia sighed. "I guess I'll wait a while and see if Kevin calls me. If he contacts you, please call me."

"OK."

After getting off the phone, Nia got up and got dressed. She'd been at the hotel since Kevin left three days ago. Her last option was to go back to the house and talk to Greg. She didn't want to, but knew he would probably be the only person who could help her locate him. She called him just before leaving out.

"Yeah, Nia?" he answered, followed by a barking cough.

"Greg, are you home?"

"Yeah, why?"

"Listen, I know I haven't been there in days, but I need a favor. If you don't want to help me, then I understand."

Greg huffed, and it forced out another cough. It lasted for at least thirty seconds.

"Greg, what's wrong with you?" she asked. "You got the flu or something?"

"No, Nia. And save your favor for someone else. I'm not interested in helping your new boyfriend. Fuck that nigga."

"Greg, what are you talking about?" she asked, as if she didn't know.

"Look, you must've forgotten that we installed those security cameras a couple months ago. I saw that you let him in. Then you gave the nigga my Polo outfit."

Greg was speaking his mind, but he was too calm about it. Normally, he would have went into a rage had he known Nia was just simply talking to another guy—Let alone inviting her ex in the house and taking his clothes.

"Greg, I'm coming to the house to talk to you."

"For what? You made it clear you want to be with him. Just let me live my life."

"So, you moved on?"

"I did," he responded. "But not with anyone else. I had three days to think about everything and when I got back from Chicago this morning, I realized that I just need to spend my last days happy."

"So, you really did go to Chicago? Why?"

"Does it really matter, Nia? You chose your ex over me so it is what it is."

"Greg, I was going to leave you regardless. You verbally abused me every day and you put your hands on me before. And for the record, Kevin and I are not together."

He groaned. "Aaah, I can't change the past, Nia, but I am sorry for what I done to you...But like I said, I'm not about to help you with this dude. You can stop by anytime to get your things, but I'm done talking about this.

Greg started coughing again and eventually hung up the phone on her.

Nia was shocked. As much as her concern for Kevin was, she worried about Greg. That, '*my last days*' remark didn't sit well with her. She felt it was her duty to at least go check on him.

She waited a couple hours then drove to their home. When she got there, she sat in the driveway for a few minutes. It was nighttime and she could see most of the house windows from the car. She noticed that the only light on in the house came from the living room. *Greg was never in the living room.*

She got out but stopped at the door. She looked through the glazing and noticed him lying down on the couch. He appeared to be sleeping, so she opened the door as quietly as she could.

However, Greg heard the screeching and he opened his right eye and squinted from the bright light. "You came to get your stuff?"

"No, I came to see what's wrong with you," she said while observing the living room. A spilled plate of Chinese food was on the floor along with several soda bottles and dirty dishes.

Greg sat up. He struggled while doing so. "I'm fine, Nia."

"Who do you think you're fooling, Greg? One thing you've always done was take care of this house. Look how dirty it is."

Greg placed his hands over his head and joined his fingers together. He looked at her and said, "Nia, go ahead and ask me your favor. You and I both know that's why you're here."

"Greg, it's not."

"Ask, please."

Nia sat on the recliner. The end table was next to her. She worked in the medical field so she immediately recognized the prescription pills sitting there. They were often given to cancer patients. She ignored it and started talking.

"Okay, Greg. First let me just confess this; when I went to Cali a couple weeks ago, it was Kevin who got shot."

"I know," he nodded. "That detective called me back. I was pissed about it, but it is what it is. Now what's your favor?"

"OK…Kevin came here not knowing his fiancé died and when I broke the news to him, he was calm at first, but then he snapped. He left out the hotel and is now in Los Angeles. I just want to see if you can call your friend again and maybe they can locate him."

"Kevin is not in danger, Nia. He went back for money. The detective is still doing his investigation and found out that Kevin was robbed when he was shot. There was a camera nearby the phone booth and it showed someone shooting him and taking a bag from him. They believe it was someone named Frank because he drove a silver Lexus. And believe it or not, word got out that a kingpin was willing to pay Kevin $500,000 dollars to take out his fiancé and her brother. I can't really say for certain, but I think he killed them. And maybe Frank shot him in retaliation. From what I hear, Frank and Slim were cool."

"And so was Frank and Mike; and Frank and Kevin. Kevin is not a killer, Greg. Frank killed them for whatever reason, and tried to kill Kevin."

"So, you really believe that Kevin didn't know his fiancé was killed? He just got shot, healed for a few days and came to you? Nia, I've been a cop for years and I've told you several times before, people do crazy shit in desperation. And don't forget all that stuff you told me about his money problems. You remember when you told me that the night you left him he was all bloody with a bag of money? I can easily tell that to the detective and have them investigate Kevin more."

"You're wrong, Greg. Kevin went down there for answers."

Greg chuckled and it turned into a cough. "Nia, Kevin went down there to get at Antonio about his money and then go look for Frank for shooting him. Trust me, Kevin

91

probably wants to find Frank before the cops do so he can shut him up. You can believe what you want to believe, but when that nigga show up on the news and his dirt gets out, don't say I didn't warn you."

"I don't even know why I came here," Nia bellowed as she stood up. "You know none of that is true. You just want to believe it so he can go to jail or get killed."

"Nia, I'm keeping my assumptions to myself. I don't have shit to do with him and I don't gain anything by snitching on him. Yeah, I'm a cop, but that's in Los Angeles. The only reason I reached out the first time was because you left without telling me the truth. The detective called me on his own this time. And I suggest you be smart enough to stay away from Kevin too before you get caught up in this shit."

"Well, just know I'm smart enough to leave you."

Nia marched to the room to gather some more of her clothes. When she came back out, she rolled her suitcase to the door. Greg was lying back down and he waited until she was almost out the door before he said something to her.

"I have cancer Nia," he said while holding back tears. "I may not be alive much longer."

"What?" She felt the adrenaline flow though her heart.

"Nia, just before you came back from Los Angeles, I went to the doctor, and that's when I initially found out. I went to Chicago because I wanted a second opinion. Once he confirmed it, I came home."

Tears immediately flooded her face. "Greg, why am I just now hearing about this? Are you going to get treatment?"

"Nia, I don't think I will. It is what it is."

"Shit," Nia mumbled as she sighed. Her compassion for Greg was overriding her feelings for Kevin. Greg was forced into his situation, but Kevin had a choice. She then remembered those words he said to her about being in love with Katrina only.

"Greg, you need to get help. Plenty of people have fought this and won."

"I need someone to help me, Nia. I don't have any strength."

"I'll help you, Greg," she sighed. "First, you need to lay back in the bed. Secondly, you can't be eating this type of food. I'll find you a place to get treatment."

He wiped a few tears away. "Thank you so much, Nia. And I'm sorry for everything I've done to you."

"It's fine, Greg. By you owning your mistakes means a lot, but my main concern is getting you healthy. I'll be here with you for as long as I need to."

"What about Kevin?" he questioned. "And I'm sorry for saying that about him. If he's really innocent, then I hope he gets whatever answers he's looking for then gets out."

She shook her head. "You know, Kevin had a lot of secrets in the past and you may be right about having some now. He made the choice to leave and he knows how to find me."

Nia walked Greg to the bed. After cleaning up the house, she went into the room and saw him sound asleep. She slipped into something comfortable and laid down next to him.

CHAPTER ELEVEN

Your Call

After leaving Jessica's house, Kevin headed over to his condo. He tried calling Nia but she wouldn't pick up. He figured that she was probably upset that he hadn't returned any of her calls. After trying a couple times, he tossed his phone onto the passenger's seat.

After getting off the expressway, he glanced up at the rearview mirror and noticed a car following him. The car looked familiar, but he didn't know why. It was too dark to see the driver.

He made a left on Atlantic and once he reached the Pacific Coast Highway intersection, he got into the left turning lane. The car followed his every move. As soon as the light turned green, he floored the gas and made a quick right turn into traffic. He glanced up and realized that the other car didn't copy his reckless driving. They were still at the light on Atlantic.

He was still afraid they would still follow, so when he got to Long Beach Boulevard, he ran the light and turned left. He turned into one of the first buildings he saw and parked in the back.

Kevin's heart rate settled after idling for a few minutes. It was at that moment he realized that he wasn't ready for confrontation. If a car following him got him that scared, there was no way he would be able to step to Antonio or Frank alone.

As he sat there, he tried to piece everything together in his head. *Was Frank working for Antonio, or was he working alone?* He just couldn't picture Frank going on a killing spree, unless he had a motive.

He decided to call Quentin in hopes to find out more.

When Quentin answered, Kevin heard wind coming through the phone. "Yo, you driving?" he asked, talking louder to speak over the wind.

"Yeah, I'm headed to L.A. What's good?"

"Man, I'm here now," Kevin responded. "I came back to find out what happened to Katrina but I don't think I'm safe. Somebody was following me a minute ago."

"Damn, Kev. You should've stayed in the A, bruh. Somehow Frank knows you're back in town and he's looking for you."

"For what?"

"Man, Frank done spread the word that you killed Katrina and Slim."

"Are you fucking serious? Everybody been filling my head up saying he did it. Matter of fact, they saying he killed Mike too."

"Yeah, I know," Quentin replied. "That's why I'm heading down that way now. I called his ass a couple days ago looking for Mike and he said he ain't seen him, then one of my other homies called me and said that Mike was dead. Frank ain't return none of my fucking phone calls either."

Kevin knew Quentin could hold his own, and anytime he was around him, or talking to him, he gained heart.

"Let me go look for him with you," Kevin said. "How long before you get here?"

"Shit, I got at least a couple hours. I'm coming up on the Bakersfield exit now. But you sure, Kev? No disrespect bruh, but I got my niggas with me and we on some shoot first shit."

"Hell, yeah. That nigga killed my fucking fiancé. I want to kill his ass and Antonio if I could. He wanted to pay me to kill her so I'm sure he probably paid Frank to do it."

"Nah, Frank may have been working on his own. And I forgot to tell you, but be careful because Kareem looking for you too. That nigga got a price on your head."

Kevin swallowed his spit and quickly looked around to make sure no one was watching him. "Who the fuck is Kareem?" he asked.

"Somebody you don't want to have beef with. Kareem and I used to slang back in the day. He and Slim were like brothers so that's why he looking for you. I can't really help you on that one because even though I don't fuck with him no more, we still fuck with the same people. Just lay low until I call you. Like I said, I'll be there in a couple hours."

"Bet."

Kevin got back on the road after he got off the phone with him. He was determined to take care of Frank no matter what. He wasn't too worried about Kareem, and since Antonio would be a difficult task, he was fine with leaving town after Frank was gone.

Frank

"I shoulda shot that muthafucka when he was coming out of Jess place," Frank complained to himself. He punched the steering wheel after Kevin cut across traffic and made a right on the Pacific Coast Highway.

He figured he was heading to his condo, but after arriving and waiting nearly ten minutes, Kevin never showed up. He was about to give up and catch him another time, but just as he cranked his car back up, Kevin pulled up to the front. He watched Kevin as he waited in the car for a few moments and when he finally got out, he followed him.

The security guard stopped Kevin and asked for his I.D. and key card. Frank was able to avoid them and take the stairs on the right. When he got to the staircase, he scrolled through his old text messages to find Kevin's unit number. "Fuck," he vented once he read that Kevin's unit was on the 13th floor.

He had to stop to catch his breath after each flight. He finally made it up there about fifteen minutes later. He quietly walked up to the door, and tried to open it, but it was locked. He knocked on the door and quickly took cover in the unlocked utility room a few doors down. He left it cracked and waited, but Kevin never came to the door.

To avoid being spotted, he decided that his best bet would be to go downstairs and wait on him. He took the elevator this time. As soon as he got off, the security guard was standing there waiting on him.

"Who are you?" the security guard questioned. "I saw you on camera knocking on someone's door. How did you get up there?"

Frank waved him off. "Get the fuck out my way," he said as he started walking out the door.

The guard trailed him, and just before Frank got out the door, he grabbed him. "I asked you a question," he said while grilling him. "We had a violent crime take place a couple weeks ago here, and that silver Lexus outside was on camera that night. I need to see some I.D. or I'm calling the cops."

Frank snatched away. "Keep your muthafucking hands off me, nigga."

The security guard trembled at Frank's demanding voice. He pulled out his radio to call for help but Frank snatched it away. He then reached into his pocket and pulled out his gun. Without hesitation, he shot him at point blank range. The guard fell but was still alive. Frank put two more in him and bolted out the door.

Kevin

After showing the security guard his ID, Kevin got on the elevator. He was about to go to his unit first, but decided to go to Katrina's. His pressed the 8th floor button.

As soon as he got off, the feeling of guilt smothered him. He felt like he was responsible for her death. Had they stuck together that night, she would probably still be alive.

He entered her apartment, and saw boxes stacked up. There was also a "Notice of Abandonment" paper on the counter. He walked past the living room and into the master bedroom. Everything was gone. While walking back towards the front of the house, he walked past the bathroom and remembered seeing that pregnancy test on her floor the night she was killed. The trash was empty, but he knew for sure that the test had two lines on it. Katrina was carrying his baby at the time of her death.

His emotions got to him, and he knelt in the hallway. Katrina was supposed to be his love forever. They were supposed to have a life together in Atlanta and be away from everything and everyone of their past.

After finally pulling himself together, he looked around the rest of the condo. All the furniture was gone and the only thing in the house were the seven boxes that were stacked in the living room. He took them down, one by one and opened them. Most of them had clothes, shoes and cosmetics, but when he picked up the last one, he found a composition book.

"Katrina's Diary," was written on the front. He sat it to the side and continued to look through the box. He found some pictures—both old and recent. He grabbed most of them and put them in a plastic bag.

Suddenly, he heard a loud bang. It sounded like a firecracker, but when he heard it two more times, he had the feeling something was wrong.

He them remembered that car he saw earlier. He picked up the bag and diary and ran out the door. Instead of taking the elevator, he chose the stairs. He took the ones in the far back which led to the back parking lot.

He ran around to the front and got into his car. Before driving away, his eyes glanced up at the entrance and he spotted a man's body slumped over near the door. Once he saw the blood, his eyes widened and terror filled him quickly. No one else was in the area, but he wasted no time getting into the car and leaving.

He sped down the expressway at nearly a hundred miles per hour. He often glanced up at the rearview mirror just to make sure he wasn't being followed. He then took the Alondra Boulevard exit and drove into Quentin's hood. Once he got close enough, he called him again.

"Yo, you here?" Kevin rushed.

"Almost bruh, what's up?"

"Man, I think Frank followed me to my condo. I heard shots when I was upstairs and when I came down, I saw the damn security guard shot dead in the lobby."

"You still in Long Beach?"

"Nah, I'm in your hood. Over there by the liquor store."

"Bet. I tell you what. I'ma call my cousin and let him know you're about to come through. Drive to that house where you and Mike used to come to. Be ready when I get there, bruh. Shit going down tonight."

"Fa sho."

As soon as Kevin hung up the phone, he came to a red light. A dark SUV pulled beside him. He turned his head to him, but the driver was looking straight ahead. A similar SUV pulled behind him. He could see his face through the rearview. Now that he observed them better, both men were Spanish and had on suits.

The light seemed like it took forever to turn green, but as soon as it did, Kevin sped off. The silver Lexus that he saw following him earlier almost ran into him, but slammed on brakes when it got caught off by one of the SUVs. He was startled, and as soon as he looked up, he realized that he was surrounded by all three vehicles.

The Lexus sped away, and before he could react, two men came from behind and drew their guns on him. They ordered him to open the car door and as soon as he did, they snatched him out and threw him in the trunk. One of the men got into the driver's seat and drove away.

CHAPTER TWELVE

Find the Truth or Die Tryin

After being tossed around from high speeds and sharp turns, the car finally stopped. He heard conversation from several men, then someone opened the trunk. He caught a glimpse of one of the men, whom he recognized, but was almost immediately hit with a sharp object. As he nearly blacked out, they covered his face while pulling him out of the trunk.

They held each of his arms and forced him to walk. They mostly had to carry him because he struggled with the boot on his foot. When they finally took the bag off his face, he found himself in a dark office. The men were laughing as they walked out the door.

He didn't know where he was. He heard the sound of faint music and the only light came from a window to his left. He looked out and saw the waves of the Pacific Ocean.

Suddenly, he heard a screeching sound and the door opened again. His eyes darted towards the men as they came back inside. They were dragging something in. Once they got all the way in and shut the door behind them, they dropped the object on the floor. It wasn't until Kevin heard the howling sounds that he realized it was a person wrapped in sheets. Blood stains covered the sheets and the men laughed and kicked him.

Another door opened and loud music swarm in and stopped abruptly when it closed. Kevin looked at the man carrying the baseball bat. Once familiarity struck, he mumbled, "fuck." It was Antonio. Antonio gave him an acknowledging smile, then turned towards the body in the sheets.

"Uncover this scum," he ordered. The men unwrapped him. His face was bruised and blood covered every inch of his body.

"Please, Antonio," the man cried. "I did everything you told me to. I made sure the clubs were running perfectly."

"Ahh, you did," Antonio replied. "But you also stole from me. It's time to pay the price."

The man continued to plead while Antonio signaled for his men to bring him the sword that was near another corner. Once in his hands, Antonio rose the sword as high as he could and came down hard on Victor's neck. The impact decapitated him.

"Pablo," Antonio said to one of the men. "Get the boat and dump his body in the ocean. Send his head to Marcus. Let that son of a bitch know he's next. Oh, and make sure you send Victor's wife, Gloria, $50,000 dollars and my condolences."

Kevin was terrified. When Antonio turned back to him, he jumped out of his seat and ran as fast as he could towards the door. His limp leg somehow gained strength and he almost got away, but tripped on the last step. The men grabbed him and held him until Antonio came.

"Don't fight it, Kevin," Antonio said to him. "You had this coming. I'm just really surprised that you came back to Los Angeles after not following my orders. You didn't think I would find you?"

Kevin took a minute to catch his breath. "Look, Antonio, I'm sorry. I couldn't get to her," he lied. "By the time I got to her apartment, Slim was there waiting on me.

He and Henry tried to kill me and I got away. I left town immediately."

Antonio tilted his hand and smile. "Oh yeah?" he asked, while looking down at Kevin's foot. "So, what's this," he said as he drilled his foot into it. Kevin cried his eyes out. The pain was so unbearable that he almost passed out, but the men saved his fall.

"Please, Antonio. I couldn't do it," he confessed. He then went on to tell the truth. "Katrina wasn't in on it at all. We confronted each other that night and came to the conclusion that we were going to leave town together. I know you thought she was the key to all of this, but she was going to leave with me."

Antonio still had the sword in his hand. He slid his finger down on it. "Kevin, this blood comes from my cousin, Victor; the man you just watched get his head chopped off. Victor worked for me for many years. I thought he was loyal so I sent him to Miami to run some clubs for me. All was good but money started coming up short. Little by little. I found out that Victor had been stealing millions from me. Not only that, he was plotting to take over. If it wasn't for this man here, I would have never known."

Kevin looked over to the other man. It was one of the men who kidnapped him and the one he recognized. Felipe was his name. He'd seen him before with Frank and Chris.

He swallowed his spit before speaking. "But, I didn't steal from you, Antonio. I told you I was going to leave town. I didn't care about the money anymore. All I wanted was for me and Katrina to go live a peaceful life."

Antonio and Felipe looked at each other and both let out a roaring laugh. "I explained to you how dangerous she was, Kevin. Yet you still wanted to leave with her? And after knowing she's dead, why come back? Clearly you knew I wouldn't be happy that I sent you to do a job and you didn't complete it."

"I know, Antonio," he said while staring at him. "I'm sure you've looked in the eyes of many people before killing them and saw lies, betrayal, and guilt on their faces…but what I saw in Katrina's eyes were pain. She loved me. Even with her brother filling her head up with accusations about me, she still didn't kill me when she had the chance. We talked and realized that it was all a coincidence and that the best thing to do was leave town— but we never got the chance."

Antonio signaled for his men to release Kevin. They still surrounded him. Antonio walked closer to him and placed his hand on his shoulder. "Kevin, you're right. I do look into the eyes of everyone I kill. Even that scumbag cousin of mine a few minutes ago. See, I can see truth in your eyes, but that doesn't give you a pass for not following my orders. You should have found a way to protect your woman at all costs and made sure the two of you never returned."

Kevin lowered his head and began to cry once again. "Just kill me," he said to him. "I probably won't be able to live with this guilt anyway."

Felipe pulled out his gun and was ready to shoot him, but Antonio stopped him. "Kevin, when my men spotted you earlier, I really thought about having them kill you there, but decided that it was best to keep you around. See, I have plans for you. Big plans. So, I'm afraid that you will be here for a while."

Kevin wiped his tears and tried to keep calm, but his stomach was starting to twist. He didn't want to die, but he also didn't want to get back into a life that he was running away from. "I just want to go home," he replied. "I don't care anymore about answers, revenge or anything."

Antonio chuckled again and turned towards Felipe. "You here that?" he asked. "What do you think, Felipe?"

Felipe still had the gun in his hand. He stared at Kevin and replied, "I say we kill this son of a bitch…And I'll do the honors."

"That'll be too easy," Antonio replied. "Like I said, I have plans for Kevin. Go join the rest of those knuckleheads by the boat. Make sure Victor's body is tied down before they drop him."

Felipe gave Kevin another stare down before walking away.

"He really wants you dead," Antonio said while looking at Kevin. "Truthfully, I don't let many men live after not obeying my commands, but I really need you to do something for me."

"Like what?"

"I will let you know when the time is right. In the meantime, you must remain in Los Angeles."

Kevin thought about the car following him earlier and the dead guard at his condo.

"It's not safe for me here, Antonio. I spoke to a friend of mine and he warned me about some people. I was even being followed."

"Kevin, I am your biggest threat. Don't worry about anyone else. My men will have eyes on you."

He gave Kevin a pat on his back and appeared to have placed something on him. He then handed him a piece of paper. "Drive to this hotel. They will know you when you arrive. Stay there until I contact you."

One of the men handed Kevin his keys back and pointed towards a road. Kevin left immediately.

When he got close to his car, he thought about Nia. He wanted to go back to her but didn't think it would be safe to try to leave. Even if he made a run for the airport he could be caught. He decided to just explain to Nia that he would be there for a while.

Nia answered nonchalantly. "Yeah, Kevin."

"Nia, I called you earlier today. I know I've been avoiding you, but I got caught on in some things. I'm sorry for everything and will be back soon, but I have to stay awhile."

"Kevin, don't bother coming back," she replied. "Or when you do, don't come see me."

He was staggered by her demeanor. He also heard a man's voice in the background. "What do you mean? And who is that in the background?"

"It's Greg."

"Greg? Nia, I thought y'all were through? What's up?"

"I don't know what's up, Kevin. You tell me. I've been trying to reach you for three days and you didn't return my calls."

"I told you I had to come down here for answers, Nia. Somehow Antonio found out I was here and he's making me stay."

"Whatever, Kevin," she sighed. "Greg is probably right about you. I don't know what to believe."

"Why is Greg in my damn business and better yet why are you with him?"

"I came back home to see if he can help me locate you and I found out that Greg is really sick. I'm here helping him. And stop lying to me. No one is forcing you to stay."

"And no one is forcing you to help him. I don't give a fuck if he's sick. He needs to be. Look at how he treated you. I'm out here getting my life threatened and you worried about him."

"Why won't you just call that detective if your life is danger? He can probably make sure you get back."

"Look, I can't. Antonio will find me."

"Bye, Kevin," she said to him. "I knew it was a mistake trying to get back into your life."

"Nia wait." She had already hung up. Kevin got into the car and slammed the door.

When he turned the ignition, he heard movement from the backseat. He held his head up to look in the rearview mirror and saw something. When he turned around to get a better look, all he saw was the gun. "Just drive," someone said.

CHAPTER THIRTEEN

Kareem

Quelle, Kareem's baby mama spotted Kevin as he was leaving Jessica's place. She followed him for a block or two until she was cut off by a silver Lexus who got behind Kevin. She ended the pursuit and went home to tell Kareem that Kevin was in town. When she got to the house, Terrell, Kareem's cousin, was inside playing a video game and smoking a blunt.

"T, where Kareem at?" she asked while jumping in front of the screen.

He moved his head over and continued to play the game. "I'on know. I think he went to Toya's house to get his hair braided. Now move out the way, I'm 'bout to score a touchdown."

She stayed there with her hand on her hip. "I don't need you to think, Terrell. I need you to KNOW where he's at. We gotta blast this fool before he leaves town again." She then cut off the TV.

"Damn, Quell! What you do that for?" he shouted. "And before who leaves? What the hell you talking 'bout?"

"I just saw that dude who Frank was telling us about. The one who shot Slim and Katrina. He was driving down Wilmington."

"Kevin?" Terrell got up from the chair and threw his beater on. "Damn, he in town that quick? Let's go holla at Kareem so we can get that fool."

Terrell made sure he had his pistol. Toya lived a few blocks down so Quelle and Terrell drove over there.

Kareem ran outside with only half of his hair braided. "Sup, cuz?" he asked.

"Man, that nigga Kev in town," Terrell replied. "Quelle think she knows where he's at."

"Call his ass up," Kareem instructed Toya when she walked outside.

He didn't answer so they just piled up in Toya's car and drove down Wilmington and back in a circle but they couldn't find him.

"I know that girl," Toya shouted as she looked out the window. They were in front of Jessica's house. She was outside with a man and a woman near a moving truck.

"Damn, where you know her from?" Kareem asked, as he checked her out in a slick way. He had to be careful since Quelle was in the car.

"That's Kevin's friend, Jessica. The one who I told you I called the other night."

His attractiveness towards her disappeared quickly. "Well, we need to run up on her ass, then. She prolly can tell us where he's at."

"Nah, I doubt it," she said to him. "She said she doesn't want anything to do with him. I'on know why, though."

"This the street I saw him on," Quelle said to them. "He was probably at her house today. We need to at least question her."

"If we question her, we got to kill her," Kareem said. "I ain't trying to get this shit too messy. I'ma wait to see if Frank catches up with him. Frank said that he would bring him to us."

"Quentin in town," Terrell said. "He called me last night asking if I seen Frank."

"The fuck he want with Frank?"

117

"He found out that Frank killed Mike so he after him."

"Man, let's pay this nigga, Q a visit. I gotta keep Frank alive until that nigga bring me Kevin and my money."

They drove over to Quentin's hood. When they pulled up, Quentin was sitting on the steps and he came to the car once he recognized them. He was a bit cautious because he hadn't seen Kareem in a minute.

"Sup, K? What cha' doing out this way?"

"I came to holla at you about Frank. I know why you're looking for him but I need you to chill for a minute. You can handle your business after he come see me."

"Man, I'on give a fuck about all that," Quentin said while sticking his chest out. "I'ma handle my business when I find the nigga. With Mike gone, my paper bout to stop. Who else gonna book these shows for me? I'on give a fuck what you or anybody else talking about. I see that nigga, I'm shooting on sight."

"Oh yeah?" Kareem said as Terrell slid him the gun from the backseat.

Quentin already knew what time it was so he took a couple steps back. He knew about Kareem and Frank working together and wondered if they had done something to Kevin since he hadn't heard from him.

After seeing Kareem's gun, he took off running. Toya threw the gear in drive and gave chase. When they got to the corner, Quentin was nowhere in sight. Kareem got out the car to look for him and Toya drove slowly on the side of him. He walked the block for a few minutes before going back to the car.

"I'ma catch your ass soon," Kareem yelled while looking towards the corner store.

"Look out!" Quelle shouted. Gunshots hit the car. Kareem jumped in and they sped away. "Turn right," Kareem said when they hit the first corner. He was familiar with the area.

As soon as they did, they saw Quentin running away. Kareem and Terrell both got out with their guns drawn. When Quentin saw them, he tried to hop the fence but struggled to get over.

Kareem fired two shots and the bullets pierced Quentin's back. His hands released the grip and he hit the ground.

"Bitch, nigga, you done lost yo' damn mind," Kareem said as he kicked him.

"Take that nigga cell phone," Terrell told him.

Kareem searched Quentin's wounded body and found the cellphone. He searched through the contacts and found two numbers for Kevin. He ran back to the car and they sped off.

"I'ma call this bitch nigga," Kareem said to them.

"He ain't gonna meet up with you," Quell replied. "He prolly knows you're looking for him."

"I'll think of something. Ain't no telling where the fuck Frank ass is at. He shoulda got to him by now."

"I'll call him," Toya jumped in. "He doesn't know that I know you. I will call him from my phone and tell him that I need to meet up with him. He will trust me since he knows that Katrina and I were best friends. Once he gives me a location, y'all can slide through and do whatever y'all need to."

CHAPTER FOURTEEN

Nowhere to Run

With the gun to his head, Kevin breathed deeply and quickly. Being faced with death twice in one night was a lot to take. This was a much worse situation than he was in with Antonio, though. Antonio's beef with him was strictly business; but with Frank, it seemed personal.

"You know, Kevin, I actually liked you at first." Frank was reminiscing on the times they used to hang out in the beginning, when Chris was alive.

"So, what happened? Greed took over?"

"Something like that," Frank said while smiling. "I think you shoulda just stuck to making them fire ass beats. I don't care what kinda money Chris offered you, you ain't built for this life."

"Chris looked out for me, though. I was just trying to be loyal."

Frank chuckled again. "Loyal? Man, niggas ain't loyal these days. See Kev, I've seen a lot of people turn on homies, family, and all. This shit ain't nothing but a game. Sometimes you win, sometimes you don't. You can't trust nobody."

"You got that right," Kevin said while taking a deep breath. "They told me you were the one who shot everybody but I didn't want to believe it at first."

"I had my reasons," Frank shrugged.

"So, what now? You got me out here to finish me off?"

"Answer this Kev," he said, ignoring Kevin's question. "How the hell did Antonio let you walk out alive? I was behind you when they kidnapped you."

"He didn'tsay," Kevin said while looking through the rearview. "He just gave me an address and told me to stay there until he contacts me."

"Turn right," Frank said to him. They went down a long road and into a wooded area. He kept the gun pressed hard against Kevin's head until he told him to turn onto a dirt road. Once Kevin came to a stop, Frank relaxed, leaned back and pulled out a blunt. "Cut the lights out."

"You gonna kill me?" Kevin cried. "Frank I don't know shit about anything. Just let me go."

"Kev, shut the fuck up," Frank roared. "You lucky I didn't take your ass to Kareem. That nigga would've made you suffer. I just wanna shoot you in the head and get the shit over with."

"But why, man? And why Katrina and the others?"

Frank leaned back again and rubbed his hands together. He and Kevin looked at each other a couple times through the rearview mirror. Frank debated if he should tell him the story, but he eventually decided to.

"I'ma start with your bitch, Katrina. That bitch was fine but was shady as hell. Her and Slim set my uncle up and killed him. You may know she was robbing niggas for her brother back in the day, but let me tell you, that bitch probably caught ten, fifteen bodies on her own. When you met her, you met her representatives."

"Representatives? What you mean?"

"Ha!" Frank chuckled. "Her other side. You didn't meet the REAL Katrina. She might've really changed, but before that, she was a cold-hearted bitch."

Kevin was raged with anger. The only thing stopping him from making an attempt to take the gun away was that Frank was too low in the seat. He figured if he could keep him talking, he could eventually make a move.

"So, why me and the others?" Kevin asked.

"Slim was simply for the money that Antonio promised you. I didn't fuck with Slim anymore but I didn't really wanna kill him either. I hoped you would've had the heart to do it, and all I would've had to do was rob your ass. But since Mike told me you were trying to leave town, I popped them then you so I could go collect. Mike could've gotten this money with me but he couldn't be trusted anymore."

"Well, it's over then," Kevin said to him while throwing his hands up. "I'm sure you got the money so go."

"I do," he smiled. "But see, I know you told Antonio something for you to still be alive. I had plans to take over Antonio's operations once I got him to trust me fully. Yu probably told him something."

"No, I didn't. I swear, I had nothing, Frank. The only reason I came back to Cali is because I wanted answers."

Frank's phone rang. He sat the gun down and looked at it. "See, that's Kareem now. Fuck that nigga. All he want is the money so he can kill me too. I ain't giving him shit. I gotta make a move out of town, so after I blast your ass, I'ma take this rental up North and lay low. I got some niggas in Sac-Town that I'ma fuck with for a minute."

A black SUV drove by and parked on the other side of the trees. Kevin noticed it, but Frank was too busy putting his phone away and picking the gun up again.

"Get the fuck out," he said to Kevin. "I can't be driving in a bloody ass car. And I'ma make it real quick," he laughed. "Just like Katrina."

Kevin opened his car door first. Frank was taking his time, so it gave Kevin an opportunity to run. He ran as fast as he could and hid behind some trees. He caught a glimpse of the SUV just as they cut their lights out.

Kevin heard Frank approaching, so he darted between the trees and ended up near a reservoir. He didn't see a way out at first, but then he saw another pathway and as he walked down it, he ended up being much closer to the SUV.

He walked over to it, hoping he could get help, but when he got closer, he realized that no one was inside. Besides the trees and reservoir, there was nothing else around. *Where could they have gone?* He thought to himself.

He backtracked so he could hopefully sneak in the car and get away, but ended up going back towards the reservoir. When he heard Frank's shouting commands, he knew he was close, so he hid behind another tree and waited.

After Frank's voice sounded faint, he slowly came from behind the trees, tiptoeing. After a few steps, he heard footsteps and looked in every direction but didn't see anyone. When he turned to walk forward again, Frank appeared. He slapped Kevin upside his head with the pistol.

"You really thought you could get away?" he asked as he pressed the gun on the back of his head. "I'ma just end this shit now."

This time it seemed impossible to escape, but Kevin waited several seconds with his eyes closed and when he opened them, he saw Frank terrified and backing away. Kevin turned around to see what he was looking at and Antonio, Felipe and two other men were standing behind them.

Frank stopped when he backed up against a tree. "Why y'all got guns on me? Shoot, this muthafucka," he shouted. "He's the—".

Felipe shot Frank at point blank range; headshot. He then raised the weapon towards Kevin, but Antonio saved him again.

"No, I told you I want him alive," he directed. "He put his life on the line to get me the truth. Frank is a piece of shit who deserves to rot in Hell."

Felipe and the other men pulled Frank's body to the reservoir and dumped him in. Antonio spoke with Kevin as they walked towards the SUV.

"I saved your life, you know. I put a recorder and a tracker on you. I followed you because I knew Frank would find you. I needed to know if he was plotting on me or not. I'm glad I found the truth."

Kevin sighed in relief. "Thank you, Antonio. Was that the reason you wanted me to stay?"

Antonio laughed. "No, Kevin, not only do I have a special task for you, but now I need you to handle the deals that I was going to give Frank. You're going to be here for quite some time."

CHAPTER FIFTEEN

Death at the Diner

Kareem slammed the phone down. "Man, I called this nigga Frank like ten damn times and he ain't answering. He needs to get at me ASAP."

Terrell shook his head. "Do you think Kev took him out?"

"Shid, I'on know. Frank usually can hold his own and I really don't know much about this Kevin dude. All I know is that I need to find his ass. Both of them. Frank needs to give me my money."

Quelle and Toya were there also. "So, is this nigga Superman or some shit?" Quelle joked. "From what I heard, he had been caught up in a couple shootouts and survived all of them. I wouldn't be surprised if he did take Frank out."

"Nah, it's the dude who owns the club by the Pier," Toya interrupted.

Kareem raised a brow. "You talking 'bout Antonio?"

"Yeah, that's him. Katrina was telling me how powerful he is. Kevin may be working for him. From what Katrina was telling me, Chris introduced him to Antonio a couple of years ago."

Kareem scratched his head. "Yeah, I know a lot about Antonio, but this Kevin shit is crazy. Chris dated Katrina a few years back, so how the fuck did she end up with him? This nigga may be more powerful than we think. He definitely got some pull in these streets."

"Or it could just be a hell of a coincidence," Terrell added. "If Kev was really about that life, we would know about him. I think Frank may lying about everything. Just think about it; he came out of nowhere and offered you a business deal. What if he was the one who killed them and trying to use us for territory? I don't trust that nigga. He's the one we should go after."

"When Frank brings me my money, then I will determine to let him live or not. For now, I need Kevin's ass buried. I still think he had some parts in this…Toya, go ahead and call that nigga up and see if you can meet him somewhere. We'll follow behind and sneak up on him on your command."

Toya

Toya called Kevin while they were all at Kareem's house. She had him on the speakerphone. "Hello?" he answered.

"Hey, Kevin. This is Toya—Katrina's old friend. Listen, she shared something with me the night that she was killed. I was hoping you and I could talk about it in person."

"What is it about?"

"I don't think talking on the phone is a good idea. You can meet me at my place."

"I don't know about that," he replied. "No offense, but I had a lot of shit happen to me in the last couple days, so I rather meet up somewhere else. How about that diner near the hospital?"

She looked over at Kareem and he gave her a thumbs up. "Okay, what time?"

"Around eight should be cool."

Kevin

Kevin waited outside the hotel before leaving since Antonio told him not to go anywhere until he contacted him. It was a risk to leave, but if Toya had information that could give him closure, it was worth the risk.

He went over to the gas station across the street and bought a bag of chips just to make sure he wasn't being followed. He came back over to the hotel and waited in the parking lot for a few before pulling off.

When he got to the diner, he drove past it and saw Toya through the window, sitting alone. After parking, he got out and walked to the front, and saw two men sitting inside a truck. They both looked at him, but he didn't think much of it and turned his head quickly.

He walked straight over to where she was sitting. "Hey, Toya," he said, sitting across from her.

"Hi, Kevin." She avoided eye contact and continued to look down at the menu.

Toya was outspoken most of the time, so her awkward behavior made him nervous. He looked around the dining room area for anyone suspicious. Two Spanish men in suits, a young couple and an elderly woman were the only other patrons inside.

"Damn, this place has gone downhill since the last time I was here," he complained. "I thought it would be busier than this."

"Yeah, everything changed when new management took over a couple of months ago. They changed the entire menu and I hate it."

She was still avoiding eye contact. Kevin also noticed that every time he spoke, the Spanish men appeared to be listening in. Whenever he would turn his head towards them, they looked away. He kept an eye on them.

Toya had her phone next to her and all she had to do was give Kareem and Terrell the word and they would come in and confront Kevin. They had plenty of guns in the car with them so they were ready and prepared for whatever.

"So, what is it that you wanted to tell me?" he asked once the waitress took their order.

She sat her phone down and held up her head with her hands. "Kevin, I'm sorry, but I really didn't have anything to tell you. I just want to know what really happened to my friend. If you know anything, please tell me."

Kevin lowered his head in frustration. "Look, Toya, I only came here because you said you have something for me. I'm caught up in a lot of things right now and this really wasn't a good time for me to meet."

"Caught up in what?" she said with an attitude. "If you know what happened to my friend, you need to tell me."

"Look, I don't know. That's why I'm here now."

She picked up her phone and texted Kareem. Kevin took noticed and decided to say something to her.

"Everything okay?"

She quickly sat it down. "Yes. Why you ask?" She tried to act as if everything was normal.

He sensed that it wasn't. "Toya, if you think I had something to do with Katrina's death then you're wrong. I loved that girl."

"Nothing makes sense right now, Kevin. Please...tell me something," she begged.

He cleared his throat and glanced back over at the Spanish men. They were still cutting their eyes at him, so he spoke lowly. "Frank killed her," he whispered. "He almost killed me, but Antonio saved my life. I'm now being forced to stay here because he has a job for me to do."

"But why would Frank kill her?"

"He said that she killed his uncle. Listen, Toya, I don't know how long y'all knew each other, but Katrina apparently been doing shit like this for a minute."

"I never questioned her about her life, but I did know she was involved in some things. But that was years ago. And why did you go to Atlanta?"

"I went because I was scared after I got shot. Once I learned that Katrina was dead, I came back looking for answers, then got caught up in this shit."

During this time, Kareem and Terrell walked in. Kevin didn't see them and they wanted to go unnoticed so they sat on the side where the Spanish men were.

Toya was starting to have a change of heart after she heard Kevin's side of the story.

"So, where is Frank?" she asked.

Kevin leaned across the table and whispered again. "What I meant when I said that Antonio saved my life is that he killed Frank just before Frank had the chance to kill me. Now, Antonio says I owe him. That's the only reason I'm here. He got me doing shit that Frank was supposed to do for him."

Toya gasped. "Oh my God, Kevin. I hope you can get out of L.A. soon."

"Yeah, I hope so too—and I hate to say it, but I'm glad Frank is gone. He killed my woman."

"So, you really miss her, huh?"

"Of course, I do. I miss her enough to jeopardize my life just to find out what happened to her. She was carrying my child when she died. That shit really hurt me.

I wish I could rewind time and save her. We shoulda never split up."

"Well, up until her death, she talked about you a lot. That was my home girl and I love her too. I've known her for years and I had never seen her go so crazy over anyone else. She was deeply in love with you. Even while she was at my house that night explaining it to me, she said that she loved you too much to kill you. Even if you were setting her up."

Kevin smiled. He never got the chance to say goodbye to Katrina, but this gave him some closure. "I 'preciate that, Toya. I think about that girl every day. I've been looking for a way to move on since I can't change the past. I think by you telling me all this, I'm able to let the past be the past and focus on my future."

Toya closed her eyes to hide her tears. She missed Katrina just as much as Kevin did. Now, everything made sense to her. She saw the truth in his eyes.

She glanced at Kareem and noticed him anxious. She picked up her phone to text him, but the waitress interrupted her and brought their food. As soon as she saw her order, she realized that it was wrong and called for the waitress but she didn't hear her. Without thinking, she got up to go get the waitress and Kareem saw this as cue to get up and approach Kevin.

Toya saw them out of the corner of her eye as they slowly approached. She knew she wouldn't be able to convince Kareem in time not to confront and possibly kill Kevin, so she had no choice but to warn him. She ran back to the table. "Kevin," she rushed. "I can't explain everything right now, but I need you to run out of here as fast as you can."

Kevin did the exact opposite of what he was supposed to do; he stayed seated. "What's wrong?" he asked.

Kareem and Terrell were getting closer. "Kareem, wait! Kevin is innocent," she cried out.

"Move Toya," Kareem replied. "It's too late for all that. I'ma bout to end this nigga now."

Kevin turned his head towards them. He didn't know them but recognized them as the two men that were sitting in the SUV earlier out front. Since they were blocking the front door, he jumped from the table and sprinted towards the back of the restaurant. Gunshots followed, hitting walls and breaking glass. It felt and sounded like a warzone.

Once the gunfire ceased, he crept up from behind the table. Blood was scattered everywhere. His eyes widened when he saw Kareem and Terrell slumped over a few tables away. Toya was still standing in the same spot, frozen.

"Hey, you okay?" he asked her.

As soon as he started walking towards her, the two Spanish men appeared. Toya was facing Kevin, and her back was to the men. When Kevin's eyes gave way that danger was still near, Toya swung her head back. She tried to run towards Kevin, but one of the men raised their gun and let out another round of gunfire. She was hit several times.

Kevin made a run for the door, but they grabbed him by his shirt. "Get the fuck off me!" he yelled.

"Kevin, calm down," the man replied. "I don't want to hurt you. Antonio sent us here to look after you. These men were associated with Frank. They were prepared to kill you."

"What about her?" he said while pointing to Toya. "She came here to share information about Katrina."

"Her blood is on your hands. You told her too much. I just need you to get out of here before the cops come. Don't meet with anyone else without talking with Antonio. He already warned you that he has eyes on you."

CHAPTER SIXTEEN

Change of Plans

"I don't know why you keep saving this kid's ass," Felipe complained to Antonio. "What's the deal with him?"

"Don't worry, Felipe. After he does what I need him to do, there won't be a need for him."

Felipe feared that Kevin would eventually be able to bridge the gap about everything and he didn't want some young kid messing up his plan. Especially not before the kilos arrived.

The bricks were coming from Angel. Angel was one of the biggest overseas suppliers they knew. He got arrested a while back for murder but got out within a few months. Now, he has hundreds of kilos to sell at a cheap price.

This was the main reason that Antonio needed Kevin. Kevin would be the one who drove the money to Angel and then drive the kilos back to the warehouse. If somehow Kevin got stopped by the cops or feds, they wouldn't be able to trace it back to Antonio because Kevin didn't know much about his inside operations.

Antonio also had several others in line with specific duties, ensuring that it would be a smooth operation.

*****

Later that day, Antonio called Kevin and gave him a location to meet him. It was in front of a closed down restaurant very close to the warehouse where Antonio would normally meet Chris. Antonio brought a few of his men and Kevin came alone. After they greeted, they searched Kevin for wires or any other devices.

"What you think, I went to the cops or something?"

Antonio laughed. "I just have to make sure."

"Well, you know my every move, don't you? I've just been sitting in the hotel waiting for your call. I am ready to get this over with."

"Kevin, I can promise you that it will all be over soon. It may take a couple more weeks, so I need you to be a little more patient. I am waiting on a phone call and then we will move out. We will be heading to the coast to make an exchange. Once the deal is done, I will reward you and you'll be free to go. For now, here's a little something extra for your trouble."

Kevin took the stack of cash that Antonio handed him, however money was no longer a motivator for him. He wanted to go home to Nia. He hadn't called her since the night Frank tried to kill him. He missed her but didn't want to get her further involved.

Antonio glared at him. "And for your troubles, I am going to let you stay at one of my houses. You can stay there until the job is done."

"Thanks," he replied sarcastically, as if that was going to make him feel any better.

Antonio ordered Felipe to drive Kevin to the house. The ride was quiet. Felipe occasionally cut his eyes over at him, but he kept his head straight and looked out the window.

Once they exited the freeway, Felipe drove down a street filled with the type of homes that Kevin only saw in movies. The streets were clean, the trees were tall, and the freshness of the air pleased his nose. They pulled into the driveway of one of the biggest houses in the neighborhood. Kevin had never seen a house so elegant.

"Whose house is this?" he asked, still trying to take in the scenery.

"Kevin, this is your home for the next couple of weeks or so. Stay here until either me or Antonio contacts you. It is fully stocked with everything you need. Food, beer, and all kinds of shit. Everything except hookers," he joked. "There's also a pool and basketball court in the back. If your ass can't swim, stay out of it. And call me if you run out of something, but otherwise stay put."

Felipe showed Kevin around the house. The inside was just as nice. He was now seeing the payoff of being a kingpin.

Before Felipe left, he showed Kevin some of the forbidden sections. Most of them were behind locked doors but he still had to let Kevin know to stay out.

Once Felipe left, Kevin poured him some vodka and sipped on it by the poolside. Despite all the events that transpired, the vodka and breeze put him in a peaceful state of mind. His past and possible future dangers were of no concern at the moment.

However, one thing on his mind besides the luxurious lifestyle was Nia. He knew he needed to call her.

Nia

After getting Greg signed up for therapy and cleaning the house, Nia left again. She was concerned for Greg's well-being but made it clear that she didn't want to continue her relationship with him. He knew it was mainly because of Kevin—and truth be told, she knew it as well.

Nia was on her way to the hotel when she received a phone call from a 310 number. She hesitated at first, but decided to answer. "Hello?"

"Nia, this me, Kevin."

She exhaled. She was relieved that he was okay, but didn't want to show any excitement. "Oh, so you finally decided to call me back, huh? Where are you?"

"I'm still here, but by force, Nia. I'm ready to come back so you and I can talk and hopefully sort things out."

"Kevin, you don't even sound like you're in trouble or there by force. I hear music in the background. Look, just tell me what's going on so I can stop worrying so much. I got a lot on my plate already."

"You still with that dude?"

"I'm helping him but I'm not staying there. I got a hotel in between the house and my job. That way I can be close by if he needs me. But where are you?"

"Look, I know it sounds crazy, but Antonio put me up in one of his houses. I don't know exactly where I'm at but we passed by that coffee shop you and I went to up the 405. We made a left on some side street and he took me to this big ass house up here."

Nia remembered the area and she wrote down what he told her.

"Have you spoken to the detective yet?"

"Nah, I'm not sweating that. Listen, there ain't nothing to worry about. As soon as I'm done with Antonio I'ma come back to Atlanta. I just called you today because I didn't like how our last call ended. Nia, just know I've been thinking about you this whole time."

"I want to believe you, Kevin, but I don't know. You always say don't worry or you got it handled, and something bad always happens. If you're in danger you need to come back now."

"Look, it's dangerous for me to still be here, but I don't know if Antonio is going to harm me. Honestly, I may be safer here than out on these streets."

"Did you find Frank?"

Kevin cleared his throat. "Look, Frank ain't a problem anymore."

"What the hell do you mean by that?" she shouted. "What happened to him?"

"He got what he deserved, Nia. Just know I'm not the one who did it."

Nia didn't want the call to end how it did last time, but Kevin was too much. "Kevin, I'm for real this time. If you can't tell me what's happening out there and when you're leaving, then don't call me. I mean it this time."

"Nia, if I could, I promise I would be on a plane ASAP."

She sighed. "I wish you would've never came back in my life, Kevin. If you knew all the bullshit you've put me through, you would see the pain I'm going through right now."

"I do, Nia. It's just—"

"Goodbye, Kevin," she interrupted.

Nia hung up the phone and sped towards the hotel. Kevin called her several times but she rejected each call.

As tears rolled down her face, she started thinking heavily about everything. She saw flashbacks of when they first met. Then she saw flashbacks of how she felt when she got the news that he had been shot.

I can't leave him if he's truly in danger, she said to herself.

There was only one way to find out. She drove down I-75 until she reached I-20 then she headed west. She didn't have any extra clothes with her, nor did she tell anyone that she was leaving. All she had was her will and determination.

CHAPTER SEVENTEEN

Welcome to the Family

Kevin was sitting in the living room and heard a knock on the door. It was a fast and heavy knock. He sat his glass down and swiftly walked to the door. When he opened it, a short, stubby, Spanish man stood in front of him. He had on a chauffeur cap, and a black suit.

"Can, I help you?" Kevin asked quickly.

The man just smiled at him and pointed to the driveway where a limo was parked out front. "Who are you here to see?" Kevin asked again. This time a little more aggressive.

The man pulled out a piece of paper. "Kay-been?" his English wasn't great. Kevin figured that he was trying to pronounce his name.

"I'm Kevin. What's up?"

The man smiled. "Oh okay, my friend. I take you to see Antonio. He'sa waiting."

"Alright, one sec." Antonio told him that he would occasionally send a driver to him if he needed him. He ran upstairs and got dressed and the driver waited in the car.

During the ride, there wasn't any communication between them. Kevin just glanced out the window as they drove on the freeway. He had no clue where they were going or who they were about to see.

About thirty minutes later, they exited the freeway and came upon an even more expensive looking neighborhood than the one Kevin was staying in.

After passing several multimillion-dollar homes, they arrived at a security gate. An armed guard was at the front and the driver rolled down the window to let him see inside. Once he saw Kevin and the driver were the only two inside the limo, he waved them through.

When they pulled up to their destination, Kevin stepped from the car, gaping at the mansion that towered over him. He had to squint as he looked up at the roof. Hedges were trimmed neatly and statues guarded the front. There was a marble water fountain that stood in the middle of the yard. On it, was a statue of a woman holding a child. The water came out through her hand and fell gently over the child's body.

Felipe came out of the house and saw Kevin admiring the statue.

"That's Antonio's only memory of his mother," he said to Kevin. "She died when he was only six years old. He remembers her singing to him at bath time."

They walked up the few stairs towards the front door, and were met by an older woman. She smiled and let them in. The floors were marble and the interior of the house looked like something out of a movie. Felipe led the way through the painting-filled hallway and into a door that opened to another huge room. That room was furnished with a bar, tables and chairs, and a few sofas. Towards the back of the room was yet another door. They walked through it and it led to the patio.

They were met with commotion.

Kevin looked at his feet and he was standing in blood, so he jumped back in fear. Felipe saw him and snickered.

"Relax, Kev. The fun is just now about to begin." Felipe told one of the men to hand him a baseball bat. The blood was coming from a wounded man. He was lying on the ground, covered in his own blood and nearly dead. Nearly identical to how Victor was weeks earlier. Felipe raised the bat and came down on the man's head at least ten times. He continued to hit him even after the cries and howling ceased.

Antonio then came into view. "Kevin, how are you?" he said while cheesing.

Kevin shrugged. He looked at the dying man on the floor. Antonio followed his eyes.

"Kevin, Kevin, I know… We gotta stop meeting like this," he joked. "You're gonna think that I am just a bad, old man. I'm really nice to those who are loyal to me, you know. This is another scum who stole from me."

Kevin didn't find any humor in it at all. The men were laughing and kicking the man as he laid there deceased. Kevin had seen enough. He stormed away and went back into the house.

"Kevin, wait a second." Antonio caught up with him. "Listen, I didn't bring you here for that. I brought you here to show you a good time around my house. You are like family now. I want you to be able to trust me."

"Trust you?" he shrugged. "Antonio, how can I trust you when all I see shit like this?"

"Name one person who I killed that hadn't crossed me first," he roared.

Kevin shrugged. "I don't know."

"Exactly. Anyone who I've killed or ordered to have killed, crossed me first. In this business, you can't be soft. You have to take care of your problems. If they do it once, they'll do it again. I make sure that I rid the problem the first time."

Seeing that Kevin was still uneasy, he wanted to give him a little encouragement.

"Kevin, in less than a week, you will be a wealthy young man. I will then give you the choice of staying in my operations or leaving. However, it is very important that you are ready for this exchange. To help you, I am going to send some guys your way; Malik and Tyrone. They're from South L.A. They are some of my toughest men on the streets. Hopefully being around them for a few days will make you feel comfortable. They will be with you when you make the exchange with Angel. I need you to not fear him. If Angel senses that you are scared, he'll either kill you or call off the deal; and if that's the case, I'll have to kill you myself."

CHAPTER EIGHTEEN

Shinin'

It only took a few days for Malik and Tyrone to help ease Kevin back in the game. They reminded him of Chris, so Kevin respected their hustle. They started off as pushers but recently moved up the chain. Both of them made a lot of money working with Antonio.

That weekend, Antonio let Kevin borrow the Benz. Tyrone was with him and told him about a club that was off Sunset Boulevard. They went and scooped Malik up and headed out there. When they got there, Malik suggested that they let valet park the car.

"We in a Maybach, nigga," Malik said to Kevin. "Let's stunt on these hoes."

The women watched them from the VIP line. Malik knew the owner so they were able to skip the line and go straight to the door.

"Y'all gonna let us in?" A group of women asked.

Malik slid his shades off to get a good look at them. "Fa' sho," he flirted as they walked in.

He bumped Kevin with his elbow. "Nigga, these hoes love swag. We gon' definitely get some pussy tonight."

Kevin nodded, but wasn't used to this type of lifestyle. He had only been to a club once or twice in his life. And outside of Nia and Katrina, he hadn't slept with any other woman. He went straight to the bar and let Malik and Tyrone chill with the women at the table.

After vibing to the music and taking down a couple of shots, he got up from the bar and walked to the restroom. He saw Malik out on the patio smoking. After walking to the other side, he saw Tyrone surrounded by a small crowd of people. He forced his way inside the crowd and saw Tyrone arguing with some dudes. They were about to throw hands and he was outnumbered four to one.

Tyrone was clearly drunk and not in any condition to fight. Kevin pulled him away.

"Man, I was about to swang on these mark ass busters," he said to Kevin. "You saved these niggas an ass-whoopin'."

Tyrone had that, 'old-school, gangsta, California' accent. All he knew was gangbanging. His pops was a legend in the hood and taught him everything he knew.

Seeing how amped up Tyrone was, it gave Kevin some confidence. "So, you gon' catch them niggas outside?" he asked.

Tyrone balled his right fist and punched his left hand. "I'ma catch them niggas real soon, but tonight since Malik got the hoes. We gon' turn the fuck up. I'm not about to let these niggas stop me from getting some pussy."

Kevin chugged the rest of his liquor down his throat and then they caught up with Malik. Malik told them that the girls were down for whatever.

"Let's take them hoes to yo place, Kev? I know Antonio got you living large in that big ass house."

"Cool," he shrugged. By now, the liquor was in his system and the women were looking good enough for him to take his mind off Nia.

They left the club about ten minutes later. They gave the women the address and sent them to the store to get some condoms and more liquor.

Once they got on the road, Kevin realized he was being followed. Once they got to a red light, Tyrone noticed the car too.

"That's probably them bustas' from the club." Tyrone grabbed his pistol and hid it under his shirt as he stormed out of the car.

Before Tyrone reached the car, they sped off. He jumped back in the car. "Man, catch them fuck niggas," he ordered to Kevin. "I swear, I'ma kill every last one of them dudes. Ain't nam' nigga finna' threaten me in my city. Fuck wrong with them niggas." They gave chase but the men got away.

However, they didn't realize that a late model black Dodge Charger followed them to the house.

CHAPTER NINETEEN

Caught Up

Antonio had Kevin meet with one of his well-known clients. The ride was long and seemed even longer coming back. He wasn't upset, though. He received a huge cut, plus it was only two days before the kilos were coming in.

On his way back to the house, he stopped to get some gas and a car pulled in at the pump behind him. The man stepped out the vehicle and stared at Kevin. Kevin took notice. He was dark-skinned, looked about mid-40s and had on 'cop-clothes'.

"Sup?" Kevin asked. The man smiled. Kevin was still in the Mercedes so he figured the man was just checking out the car.

"Nothing much," the man finally replied. "I'm just admiring your whip. All I can afford is this Charger I got."

"That's a nice ride, though," Kevin responded.

"Yeah, I know, but not like yours. What kinda work you do, if you don't mind me asking?"

Kevin looked down and chuckled. "Well, I actually do mind," he said as he stopped the pump.

"My bad, young fella. I forget you young cats don't really like to hold a conversation with anyone. Have a nice day."

Kevin got into the car and drove off.

He made one more stop and when he finally made it to the house, the same Dodge Charger from the gas station was parked in front of the driveway. The man was looking down like he was gathering paperwork. Kevin had his gun on him so he got out and walked to the driver's side with confidence.

"Yo, why you following me?"

The man rolled the window all the way down and raised his head. He smiled from end to end before talking. "I'm here for you, Kevin."

Kevin took two steps back and tensed up when he saw a laptop and scattered paperwork in the man's front seat.

"What do you want with me?" he asked.

"Kevin, you may not remember me, but my name is Detective Caldwell. I spoke to you when you were in the hospital. Things calmed down at first, but now they have picked back up. We've had eyes on you for a few weeks. Really longer than that, but ever since you came back, I've been following you. I have to ask you a few questions and that will determine how much trouble you are in."

Kevin broke into a cold sweat. His knees bounced and legs felt like they were as light as feathers. His breathing was quick and uneasy. He not only feared what kind of trouble he was in, he feared that Antonio could have eyes on him and spot a cop in his driveway.

"We have to talk somewhere else. It ain't safe for me to do it here."

"I agree," Detective Caldwell replied. "Meet me at that coffee shop off of 118 and Woodley. The one you went to the other day for a cup of dark roast. You got twenty minutes to get there."

Detective Caldwell drove off.

"Shit, shit, shit!" Kevin screamed as he jumped up and down. This detective knew too much about him. He took all the money and dope out of the car and into the house and stuffed it in a closet where Felipe showed him to hide everything in case something went down. He then checked the house to make sure nothing illegal was out in view.

*****

Caldwell was already inside of the coffeeshop when Kevin pulled up. Kevin sat across from him. Caldwell took a sip of his coffee and said, "they need one of these on every corner. I would choose this over the national chains any day."

"Can we get to the point?" Kevin interjected.

Caldwell took one last sip. "Sure... Kevin, I am the original detective that was assigned to your case when you were shot back in December. All fingers pointed to Nate 'Slim' Jones as the shooter, but he was murdered that same night. We had no other leads, and when you left town, the case went cold."

"If this is about who shot me, I'on know who did it." Kevin's eyes darted to the left and right as he spoke.

"So, you're going to lie to me in my face?" Caldwell questioned. "Kevin, I know you know who shot you. You also know who killed your fiancé and her brother."

Kevin sat back while the detective pulled out his phone. He went through a few text messages.

"You see, I got a call from a buddy of mine and he knows a former cop by the name of Gregory Smith. You may know him as Greg. I called him up and he told me the story about both of you being in love with Nia. I have her name down as Nia Franklin. He said that Nia left him to be with you back in early January. You were healing from the gunshot wounds and came here before you even recovered."

Kevin shook his head with a disgusted look on his face then he interrupted him. "I came here to find answers. And since Greg want to tell you everything, did he tell you how his punk ass used to hit on Nia and call her out her name?"

Caldwell wasn't a pushover and he could see that Kevin wasn't really a gangster. "I'm not a domestic social worker, Kevin. I am a damn detective. I investigate murders. The point is, Greg said that Nia came home and asked if he could call up some friends in L.A. to look for you. I just so happened to be the one working your case so I recognized your name immediately. We spoke about Frank, but before we could really tie him to anything, we found his remains in an acid lake."

"So, what cha' trying to say? I didn't kill him if that's what you're thinking."

Caldwell smiled. "We know that, Kevin. We just need you to tell us who."

Kevin had to keep an aggressive attitude to hide his lies. "I'on know shit. If you're gonna charge me with something then do it. It won't hold up in court. I'm not a killer."

"Kevin, I can match you on the scene of several murders. I want you to listen to this report and tell me if one thing on it is false. I am pretty confident that you won't be able to do that."

"Go ahead," Kevin said with confidence.

Caldwell pulled out the report and read it to Kevin. He skipped over the murders of Slim, Katrina, Mike and Henry, and read every connected murder that happened since Kevin came back to Los Angeles.

"January 29th. Victor Fernandez's body was found on the shore next to a nightclub owned by Antonio Rivera. He was decapitated. Nearby traffic cameras show a rental car checked out to a Kevin Dawson near Mr. Rivera's club.

"February 1st. Quentin Miller was found wounded in an alley near his grandmother's home. He died from his wounds shortly after. His cellphone was not on him but we were able to get records of his last few calls. Two were to Franklin Armstrong, aka, Frank; and Xavier Haywood, aka, Zay. The last call was to Kevin Dawson.

"February 3rd, Franklin Armstrong's body was found in a reservoir near 7th Street. His body was severely decomposed, but we were able to determine that he died from gunshot wounds. It was determined he'd been there a few days."

"February 4th. Kareem Anderson, Terrell Brooks, and LaToya Bryant were all found shot to death in a diner. Footage shows Kevin Dawson sitting at a table with LaToya Bryant before she was shot by two unidentified shooters. Phone records show that Mr. Anderson had been in contact with Frank. Phone records also show that Ms. Bryant was in contact frequently with Katrina Jones back in the day."

"Last, February15th. Ramon Augustus… Body found in a wooded area near Antonio Rivera's estate. Surveillance footage at a security gate shows Kevin Dawson and Jose Lopez entering the private area of Mr. Rivera's estate in a limo."

"I can name a few more, if you like," Caldwell said to him. "A security guard was killed at your old condo building. Your fingerprints were found in Katrina's unit. Franklin's were found in the building also. "

Kevin lowered his head. Caldwell seemed determined to find the head guy responsible for everything. He decided to tell.

"Look, Antonio is behind all of this," he confessed. "He's the reason for Katrina's death and everybody else. Whatever else you need me to tell you, I will."

"That's what we figured," Detective Caldwell said to him while putting the report back in his briefcase. "I want to make a move on Antonio, but I just need help catching Angel first. He's the one who is bringing the keys across the water."

"Why not just take him in now? Especially if you know he's responsible for all these deaths."

"Listen, Angel is a dangerous man and we can only get to him through Antonio. If they have as many kilos as we think, we're talking millions worth of drugs. Probably closer to half a billion. We need our hands on the money and drugs. Antonio has a lot of people working for him and he can fight his way out of the murders, but if we catch him red-handed with the dope, there's no way out of that."

"Well, I'on want no parts of this," Kevin replied, waving his hands. "Y'all already know more about the drug deal than I do. Just find a way so I can go home safely. I have a lot to patch up with Nia."

Detective Caldwell snickered. "I'm afraid that it's too late for that, Kevin. You can either go through with this or either explain to the judge why your name is tied to every murder on that report that I read to you."

"So, you gonna frame me for this shit?" Kevin slouched back in the chair and shook his head frustratingly. "You just said you know Antonio did it."

"I don't want to do that but if I have to, I will. I just need your help. We have all the information we need except for the location. We will put a tracker on you and once you're near the drugs and money, we'll move in. I need you to not tell a soul about this, though. My department is trying to close this deal secretly. We don't want to get the feds, or any other local agencies involved. I promise you, after this, we will have Antonio and Angel and you will be free to go."

*****

Kevin went straight to bed when he got home. The fear that things wouldn't go as planned took over him. He was sure that either he would go to jail or get himself killed. Every bit of regret flooded him.

Suddenly, there was a knock at the door. He looked out the window and saw a car parked in the driveway. That car looked familiar, but to be certain, he ran to the door. As soon as he opened it, his eyes widened.

"Nia?" he declared. "How did you get here?"

"It doesn't matter Kevin," she said while forcing her way in. "Get all your belongings. We are about to go home."

She was the last person he expected, but was the only person that he wanted to see.

CHAPTER TWENTY

Raphael

Antonio poured two shots of cognac while sitting in the back of his limo. One for him and one for Raphael, as they were about to celebrate. He was hours away from making one of the biggest drug deals in history. As long as everyone was in the right position, no one could stop him.

The back door opened and the driver let Raphael in. He sat next to Antonio and they embraced. Raphael was a clean-cut, Spanish man, probably in his late thirties. He was dressed just as clean as Antonio was. Antonio handed him the drink. "Raphael, does that son of a bitch, Angel, know you are in town?"

"Who, my father? No. He thinks that I am in London. He should be arriving at LAX around ten this morning. The ship will be here no later than four this afternoon."

Raphael and Antonio had been plotting in secret for a while. The plan was too take Angel's keys, but keep the money. Antonio and Angel are half-brothers but were never really close—and from what Antonio knew, Raphael hated his father so calling him up to set him up was easy.

"One thing I know about my father is that he is going to want to see the cash before he releases the cocaine."

"Yes, I know," Antonio nodded. "I have a young kid named Kevin who is going to bring the money in from a different location. Once Angel's men release the bricks, you come out the car and shoot him. Make sure he's dead. As far as Kevin, I will let him take the keys back to the warehouse. After that, I won't need him anymore. I promised him a couple million. The kid has done a lot for me, but Felipe wants me to take him out…What do you think?"

"Overall, it'll be easy," Raphael sighed. "There will only be a few guys on the ship. All we have to worry about is the three or four that will be riding in the truck with my father. As far as the kid, Kevin, I say take him out. If you cared for his life, I'm sure you wouldn't even have to question it."

"I'll think about, Raphael. Kevin was kinda forced into this….And as far as other my men, I will have at least ten of my best shooters with me. We are guaranteed to take all of them down."

"No, bring only two or three of your best men. Maybe have an extra one on the roof but if Angel sees a lot of men, he will call off the deal. Trust me, my father will be an easy hit. It only needs to be a couple of us."

CHAPTER TWENTY-ONE

Know your Role

"We're talking pure cocaine for twenty a key," Antonio said to his men at the warehouse. "That's a steal—and that's exactly what we are going to do. I never told any of you this, but Angel is my brother; half-brother. I am working with his son, my beloved nephew to take him down. I will be the biggest Cartel in the world once this is over. And all of you will be paid a pretty penny."

It was a room of nearly fifty men, including Raphael. All of them whom Antonio trusted. He had to hand select three men to take with him and Felipe was one of them.

Felipe would be the sniper and Antonio would ride to the dock with him and get him in position. The other two would drive a separate vehicle and be the ones who initially greet Angel. Raphael would be laying low in the backseat with them. The other forty or so men would be at the secret location, on standby. They would be ready to pop off if needed.

Once the meeting was over, he called Kevin. Knowing that Raphael nor Felipe were not too fond of him, was the main reason Kevin wasn't invited to the meeting. He gave Kevin the address and told him to be there four o' clock sharp.

Kevin

Kevin wrote down the address and looked at the time and it was a few minutes after ten. Nia was on the hotel bed sound asleep. He promised her that he would go to the authorities on Antonio and Detective Caldwell. After Kevin told her everything, she felt that Caldwell may have a plot of his own.

Kevin got out the bed and looked at himself in the mirror. He started trembling. Antonio's voice reminded him of how powerful he was. He knew his best bet was to go through it as planned and rely on Caldwell and his officers to arrest Antonio. It was no longer about the money for him—he just wanted to get out alive.

Kevin plugged the address into his phone. It was about an hour away. It was still early, but he needed to sneak out before Nia awakened. He picked out some clothes from his bag and got dressed in the bathroom. Once he came out, he glanced over at Nia again. Sound asleep. He tiptoed to the door, carefully opened it, and left.

CHAPTER TWENTY-TWO

Ride or Die

Nia rolled over and wrapped her arms around Kevin as he slept. After searching for him for more than a week, she was able to find him through some connections. She made him get all of his belongings out of Antonio's house and they were about to head home the next morning. There was something strange about Detective Caldwell so she did want Kevin to contact him nor the local authorities. She didn't like the fact that he was putting Kevin in harm's way by going through the drug deal.

To be certain, while Kevin was asleep, she texted Greg. He told her that Kevin was no longer wanted and his original case was closed. All of the murder cases that Caldwell told him were probably something he investigated on his own.

That put a smile on her face. All she needed to do now was to get a good night's sleep to prepare herself for the long drive back to Atlanta. She made the first trip in just under two days by herself, but this time she planned on getting back even quicker since Kevin would be with her. She would do her best to keep him away from Cali for good this time.

She finally drifted off to sleep.

*****

Nia stretched and yawned as the sunlight crept in their hotel. After adjusting her eyes to the light, she rolled over to put her arms around Kevin, but this time, her arm fell flat on the mattress. She jumped up, almost in a panic. "Kevin?" she yelled. After not getting a response, she rushed to the bathroom since the light was on, but Kevin wasn't there either.

"Kevin..." she sighed. She tried to call him but the phone kept ringing.

She tried to keep her cool, hoping that he just went out to get some breakfast or something, but after waiting nearly an hour, she knew it was something else. As she was putting on some clothes to go look for him, she saw a paper on the ground. It had an address on it, belonging to a port. She knew then that Kevin had gone through with the deal.

CHAPTER TWENTY-THREE

Waist Deep

Kevin arrived at the warehouse about ten minutes earlier than he was supposed to. He sat in the car, breathing heavily, trying to build up some courage to go through with it. He thought of the consequences if Antonio found out he was working with Detective Caldwell. He had to be prepared to get out as soon as the slightest thing popped off.

He parked his car directly behind the warehouse, away from cameras like Antonio instructed. The garage door was unlocked so he lifted it up and saw the truck parked a few feet away. On the outside, the truck was just a plain, typical delivery vehicle, but on the inside, ten briefcases filled with one million apiece, lay right in front of his eyes.

As he sat there admiring the money, he saw a shadow dart past him. It came from the far-right corner near the garage door where he walked in. He scanned the place but didn't see anyone. *It could've been a reflection*, he thought to himself.

After surveying the warehouse, no one appeared so he brushed it off and sat in the truck. Antonio called minutes later, telling him to head to the dock.

Antonio

As the ship rolled in, Antonio and Felipe were on a hill near the dock. He was about to get Felipe in position on the roof so he could be on standby. The other two men were at the dock, ready to assist with the kilos.

A black, SUV with dark tint pulled up to the port next to Antonio's men. Several people got out including Angel. Felipe was armed with a rifle and a scope. "Should I get on the roof now?" he asked Antonio.

"Yes. Wait on my command, though. I am going to wait to make sure that he has the kilos. The ship should be docked any minute now. If Raphael can get a good shot, then you don't have to do anything."

Antonio walked back to the car and made a phone call while Felipe climbed the ladder and got into position on the roof. Minutes later, Antonio carefully climbed the ladder, trying not to make a sound, but when he got to the top, the ladder shifted, causing a clang.

Felipe turned around when he heard it. "You scared the shit out of me," he joked. "Are you staying up here until it's done?"

Antonio didn't answer him and Felipe turned around to focus in on Angel through the scope. He walked towards him while he was lying down then squatted next to him.

"So, Felipe, how important is loyalty?"

"What do you mean, Antonio?" he responded, still in aim. "Loyalty is everything, right? At least that's what you told me."

"Precisely." Antonio had a revolver with a silencer on it. He adjusted it while Felipe's back was still turned.

"You see, I am very loyal, Felipe. The problem is, I was loyal to the wrong things. Why be loyal to people when they want your position? Want you dead?"

Felipe blinked nervously a few times. He turned around and saw the barrel of a gun in his face. "Whoa Antonio," he cried. "What's going on?"

"I think you know exactly what's going on. I just so happened to beat you to it. Goodbye, Felipe."

Antonio put the gun in between his forehead and pulled the trigger. The impact caused Felipe to fly off the roof.

Antonio walked to the edge to get one last look at him. He hoped that by killing Felipe, it would send a message to anyone else who thought they would be able to plot against him.

He looked around at Angel and the others. They were far enough to have not heard the commotion. He then put his gun away and put his shades on and went down to meet them. As soon as he got close enough, he saw Kevin pulling in. He threw up his index finger, instructing him to wait there. He wanted to make sure that everything was legit so he pulled in first and parked where the crowd was. Antonio's men gathered around him and Angel's men did the same with him.

Antonio counted ten armed men who were with Angel. Now that Felipe was dead, Antonio only had two armed men. "Where the fuck is Raphael?" Antonio grumbled to himself.

Angel took a few steps towards Antonio but kept a safe distance. "You got the money, Antonio?"

"You got the good?" Antonio returned.

"Of course," he said while looking back at the ship. "This boat ain't a cruise ship, ya know."

Antonio still searched for Raphael. "I need to see the drugs," he said to Raphael.

"Come on, little brother, where's the trust?" Angel said with his arms spread wide and smiling. "I am here to sell you something so as soon as the money is in my hand, we can get this deal over with."

Antonio pointed in the other direction. "My driver is parked up front."

Angel saw the truck. He then showed the kilos and Antonio looked around impatiently as Raphael was still nowhere to be found. This was the first time he didn't have a plan B.

"Looking for someone?" Angel grinned. Suddenly, a door opened from the same truck that Angel got out of and Raphael appeared. He walked over to Angel and put his arm around his shoulders.

"We haven't seen you in over ten years, Antonio," Angel said to him. "Do you really think my own son would turn on me?"

More cars rushed in and they were all with Angel. Unfortunately, Antonio wasn't prepared and there was no way out of this.

He did have two of the most loyal men ever, though. Without hesitation, they fired their weapons. Angel's men tried to get him to safety.

Antonio took cover and prepared for a final battle. Once he saw Angel retreating, he aimed his gun carefully, and pulled the trigger. It was a perfect hit. Angel and the two men who retreated with him were struck.

Angel's men quickly retaliated, and Antonio's two men were gunned down immediately. Antonio came into view and let off every round he had. He hit a couple of them, but ultimately took a shot to the head.

Police and feds finally rushed in and took down all the survivors.

Detective Caldwell

Detective Caldwell and his men emerged from one of the trailers. He slammed his fist into the wall and eyed each one of his men with him. "How the fuck did the feds know about this?" he screamed. "We were supposed to get the money and kill all of those fuckers."

All Caldwell wanted was the money, but someone had informed the feds. He made sure to not disclose this to anyone else except his seven loyal men. He carefully gathered and destroyed all evidence so no one else would find out his plan. They were equipped with enough guns to take out Angel and Antonio's crew, however, that plan was ruined when the feds came.

He spotted Kevin driving away. He didn't have time for all his men to sneak out of the trailer, so he went and followed Kevin himself.

Kevin

Once all the officers rushed in like Caldwell promised, Kevin quickly backed the truck away and took it back to the warehouse like Caldwell instructed.

He saw with his own eyes Antonio getting shot dead. With all his enemies gone, no one would be after him. All he needed to do was drop off the truck at the warehouse and get into his car to go pick up Nia. She would definitely be upset knowing he went through with the deal, but seeing that he came out alive, he knew that she would eventually get over it.

When he arrived at the warehouse, he pulled into the garage door and parked the truck in the far back corner. On his way back to his car, he decided to call Caldwell to let him know that the truck was there and that he was leaving.

As soon as he dialed the number, he heard a phone ringing from within the warehouse. Caldwell then emerged from the other side of the truck. Kevin was startled, but once he saw him, he relaxed. "Everything should all be back there," he said to him. "I didn't touch a thing."

Caldwell showed no emotion. When Kevin looked down, he realized that Caldwell was holding a gun. He pointed the gun towards the back of the truck. "Open it," he ordered.

Kevin obeyed his command. As soon as the latch was unlocked, Caldwell shoved him out the way and pushed the door up. Once he laid eyes on the briefcases, he raised the gun up at Kevin again.

"Aye man, I did everything you told me to do. I drove off once I saw your men swarm in."

"You think those were my men?" Caldwell chuckled. "No, Kevin. Somebody fucked my plan up. My team was supposed to get the dope from Angel and kill them all, but somebody called the local authorities."

Kevin's eyes widened. Nia's theory was right. And now with the money right there and Caldwell being the last person between him and getting out of there alive, he put his hands up and backed away slowly. "The money is all there, sir. I didn't tell anyone about this. I can walk out alive and you can take the money and go."

"I don't think that's possible, Kevin. Someone talked. See, once I found out that you were a link to Antonio, I destroyed all the evidence and built a bogus case around you to get you to talk and go with the plan."

"Well, it looks like it worked," Kevin said. "What else do you need?"

"I need you dead…just like the others are. If I let you walk, they may be able to trace something back to you and come look for you. Although I'm about to retire on an island somewhere, I can't have you snitching on me. I already got a story lined up to tell them what happened with you and the money."

"So, you used me?" Kevin said as his eyes turned to find any area to run to. "You were going to kill me even if you the feds didn't show up, huh?"

"I don't know," he shrugged. "That would have depended on how my men felt—but with them still at the port, and possibly getting questioned, I gotta clean this shit up. If they go down, I go down and vice versa."

Caldwell wanted to make sure the money was really there before turning the gun on Kevin. He started opening the briefcases one by one, and as he confirmed money was inside them, he placed them on the ground. His car was just outside the garage door. After taking care of Kevin, all he would need to do was load them in the back of his vehicle and drive away.

Kevin had one chance to escape and that was to sprint past Caldwell while he was distracted with the briefcases. As soon as Caldwell placed one of the briefcases down, Kevin rushed by, and knocked him to the ground in the process. The gun slid across the floor, and Kevin had the opportunity to get it, but he just wanted to get away. He to the garage door and tried to lift it up, but it was locked with a padlock. Caldwell must've locked it when he came inside.

There was only one other way out and it was through the side door. He ran in the direction of it, but couldn't see it since there were other trucks blocking the view. Once he got closer, he heard the door open and saw the sunlight shine in. He stopped and took cover. Either Caldwell went out or someone else came in.

He ducked and crept between the trucks. He stopped when he saw a shadow dart past him. Before he could make another move, he felt the gun on the back of his head.

"I admire your effort Kevin, but this looks like the end of the road for you. Nothing personal, but I can't let you live with everything you know."

Kevin didn't bother to turn around. He stood there, still ducking, and closed his eyes. Suddenly, he heard two shots, followed by a loud thud.

He turned slightly and saw Caldwell lying flat on his stomach. A pool of blood quickly flowed out.

He looked over at the shooter. It was Nia. He took a deep breath and comfort followed. He ran up to her and hugged her.

"See, I told you I had your back," she said as boldly as she could, still holding the gun.

"Shit, Nia," he said while still gasping for air. "You saved my life. How did you get here? And where the hell you get a gun from?"

"You left the address on a piece of paper this morning, and as far as the gun, I did date a cop for almost two years, you know. One good thing he taught me was how to use one."

"Look, we need to get out here," he said to her.

Kevin ran towards the door almost leaving her behind. Nia initially followed, but she suddenly stopped. He didn't notice it until he was right at the door.

"Nia, let's—"

He stopped in midsentence when he saw her grabbing the briefcases.

CHAPTER TWENTY-FOUR

The Aftermath

Kevin didn't tell Nia where they were heading. All she knew was that it was eight in the morning and she found herself pacing down the busy terminals at Hartsfield-Jackson airport.

"Bae, just tell me where we're going," she said, tugging on to him.

Finally, he gave her, her plane ticket. A first-class flight to New York. "What's in New York, bae?"

"You'll see, just relax."

Relax was what she definitely wanted to do. Her eyes were heavy. She had only gotten six hours of sleep after their thirty-five hour drive from Los Angeles to Atlanta. Now, they were about to travel again.

After boarding the plane, she snoozed up in her neck pillow. Once in the air, she dozed off, only to be awakened by turbulence. She glanced over at Kevin and he was pulling out a book from his bag.

"What's that?" she asked.

"Something I think that may help complete my journey."

The title read, Katrina's Diary. Kevin initially thought of it as invading her privacy, but he never got the chance to know the real Katrina. She promised to tell him her life story, but unfortunately she didn't live long enough to do so.

Nia put her hand on the book before he opened it. "Bae, I think you should read that another time. Maybe when you know you're at peace with everything."

"You're right," he nodded. He put it away and rest his head on the window while Nia rested on him. They slept until they touched down in New York.

They got into a taxi and drove into the city. This was their first time there, but Kevin had directions to a building like he had something planned. Nia just gazed out of the window and took in her surroundings. Despite the chaos and traffic, she was at peace.

The driver dropped them off at a building off of Broadway. "You're still not going to tell me what we're doing?" she asked.

"You'll see in a few minutes. I promise."

As they entered the building, Nia scoped the place out. The plaques on the wall revealed that it was a record company. Kevin pressed the elevator button and they rode it to the 22nd floor. As soon as they stepped off, they were surrounded by more plaques and portraits of famous musicians. Directly in front of them was a glass door and they both walked through it. Kevin told Nia to have a seat and that he would be right back.

As Nia sat down, she browsed her phone and didn't notice the glass doors opening again. Someone called her name. "Nia," the female's voice said gently.

She looked up and Jessica's was standing in front of her went her arms extended. She jumped up and hugged her.

"Aww, girl I missed you so much!" Nia couldn't stop smiling. "Girl, look at you," she complimented.

Jessica had a completely new look and a glow on her. She hadn't dressed this nice since her graduation party that Kevin threw for her. Now it had become an everyday occurrence. Jessica was finally out of her shell.

Nia still felt bad about how everything went down between them and now that they were face to face again, she wanted to apologize in person. "Listen, girl, I'm so sorry about how things went between us."

Jessica quickly interrupted her. "Nia, no apology is needed. You did what you felt was right. By me being alone, it motivated me to get something going. I focused hard to become a good recording engineer and it paid off. Plus, we're all alive so there is nothing to worry about."

Kevin came back from the restroom and greeted Jessica. He noticed her new look too. "I see ya' Jess. Must got you an NYC dude now or something. I love the new look."

She smiled. "Something like that."

"Well, I'ma let you two talk," Nia said to them. She left and checked out more wall memorabilia."

Kevin and Jessica went to her office. "Kevin, are you really done with everything now?" she asked him.

He snickered. "I am," he said confidently. "I flirted with death many times while I was there. It's over now. And even though Katrina isn't alive to tell me her story, I found a diary of hers. I may skim through it."

"Well, I hope it gives you the complete closure that you are looking for. I don't want to see you going crazy if you discover something new."

"Naw, Jess," he laughed. "I'm good. She promised me that after we moved, she would answer any questions that I had. Maybe this diary will just let me get to know the real Katrina. See her life as she matured into the beautiful woman that I met."

Jessica's nodded. "Oh, shoot," she said, interrupting her thought process. She looked at her watch. "I have a quick meeting to get to, Kevin. We can catch up later this afternoon?"

"The meeting can wait a few minutes," a firm voice said from the office around the corner.

Kevin wrinkled his face in confusion but it turned into a smile. The award-winning, music producer, K.P. walked into the room with them.

"Kevin, I would like you to meet my fiancé, Kendrick Peterson," Jessica said when K.P. put his arm around her.

"That's what's up!"

K.P. extended his hand to Kevin. "Kevin, Jess let me hear all of your beats. We need to do business soon."

"I'm down. Just get at me. I'm about to get back in business with my boy, Zay again."

"I'll be waiting," K.P. said while smiling. He grabbed some papers and walked away. Jessica stood up.

"Well, Kevin, I have to get into this meeting. How long are you in town? Maybe we can catch up this evening or possibly tomorrow?"

"Let's do tomorrow," Kevin said. "Nia and I will probably head to the hotel and get some sleep."

After Jess closed her office doors, Kevin went back in the lobby with Nia. Her sleepiness had worn off and she was excited to be in New York.

"So, what's next? You're about to take me to see the Statue of Liberty or Times Square?"

He put his arm around her shoulders. "How about we rest."

She sighed but gave in. "Alright, Kevin. I guess we got plenty of time."

"We sure do. I mean, we got the time and money now to go wherever we want. I was thinking you and I go on an island for a few days."

"How about a few weeks?"

"Even better."

And just like that, Nia's excitement wore off as soon as she step foot in the hotel. She slipped into her night gown and fell asleep within a matter of minutes.

Kevin couldn't sleep, so he sat in the recliner and watched his beautiful queen as she slept. Had it not been for her will and determination, he wouldn't be here. He was forever thankful.

Kevin reached in his bag and picked up Katrina's diary. He leaned back in the recliner, and got himself comfortable. Before he opened it, he promised himself not to trip no matter what he saw. He understood she had a lot of things in her past that wasn't pretty.

As soon as he opened the first page, his thoughts were confirmed. Entry 1 was labeled, "My First Kill."

Kevin knew he was in for a wild ride.

THE END

Don't forget to visit

www.ronleath.com for updates

and new releases!

Facebook: Author: Ron Leath

Instagram: ronleath

Email: info@ronleath.com

About the Author

Ron Leath was born in Jacksonville, FL and currently lives in Dallas, TX. An unashamed believer in God, a family man and a hard worker, Ron looks to inspire others with his writing. He has been married since 2008 and he and his wife are raising two beautiful children. His mission is to entertain readers with his creative fiction and also show the world that if you believe in yourself, you can accomplish anything.

Be sure to visit www.ronleath.com for updates and new releases!